"Tough Love"
M/M Gay Romance

David Horne

This book is intended for Adults (ages 18+) only. The contents may be offensive to some readers. It may contain graphic language, explicit sexual content, and adult situations. May contain scenes of unprotected sex. Please do not read this book if you are offended by content as mentioned above or if you are under the age of 18.

Please educate yourself on safe sex practices before making potentially life-changing decisions about sex in real life. If you're not sure where to start, see here: http://www.jerrycoleauthor.com/safe-sex-resources/ (courtesy of Jerry Cole).

This story is a work of fiction. Names, characters, businesses, places, events and incidents are the products of the author's imagination or used in a fictitious manner and are not to be construed as real. Any resemblance to actual persons, living or dead, or actual events is purely coincidental. Products or brand names mentioned are trademarks of their respective holders or companies. The cover uses licensed images and are shown for illustrative purposes only. Any person(s) that may be depicted on the cover are simply models.

Edition v1.00 (2021.01.25)

http://www.DavidHorneauthor.com

Special thanks to the following volunteer readers who helped with proofreading: Bob, RB, Blue Savannah, Big Kidd and those who assisted but wished to be anonymous. Thank you so much for your support.

Chapter One

"Come on, Mark!" Stevie slumped in the passenger seat, arms folded with a scowl. "You can't keep giving me the silent treatment. You've been doing it since we left the school."

Mark's hands tightened on the wheel.

"I'm not giving you the silent treatment, Stevie." That was partly true. "I'm just trying not to get too angry. I don't want to say something I'm going to regret."

"It's not my fault! They threw the first punch! I was only defending myself."

"I get that, Stevie, but the fact is, you said you wouldn't get into any more fights..."

Stevie snorted rudely, brushing his blond hair out of his eyes.

"Can I help it if they keep coming to me looking for problems? I was minding my own business at lunch when they jumped me!"

Mark knew that, but he was still angry. Stevie had promised him the week before, after the fifth time that semester when Mark had been called in to take Stevie home because he had been suspended again. It was only after the second time that Mark managed to get the bullies themselves suspended, as it only seemed to be Stevie being targeted. It was like teachers and students didn't care about him.

Mark hated it when people lumped the kids of bad people in with the ones responsible. It was not fair to the children. They were just as innocent; Mark had seen it too many times. And it still made him sick to know it was still happening.

4

Stevie was only thirteen, his sister ten. They had only been ten and seven when their father was arrested as a serial killer. Now everyone looked at Stevie and Christy thinking they were complicit in all of it. Mark didn't think he would be able to get anyone to change their minds anytime soon.

It was unfair and Stevie was getting the brunt of it right now. Teenagers were just the worst.

"I hate school." Stevie grumbled. "I get blamed for everything."

"I'm not blaming you."

"Sounds like you are."

Mark took a deep breath and let it out slowly. The news from the principal about one of the kids had spooked him.

"I'm just scared, Stevie. One of the kids who jumped you, he was carrying a knife."

If the track coach hadn't come upon them then, chances were that kid would have used the knife. That sent shivers down Mark's spine. And the bastard principal didn't want to call the cops until Mark threatened to report him to the school board and stood over him while he made the call. It was almost like the guy didn't want the kids to be caught.

Who would turn a blind eye to that? That school was more of a screw-up than Mark realized. He had only kept Stevie and Christy at places they were familiar with, not wanting to change schools. Now he was beginning to regret it.

Mark knew he was taking on a lot when he agreed to foster the brother and sister pair. Christy had been incredibly withdrawn and didn't speak for nearly six weeks, and Stevie had been sullen and

5

combative. It had taken a lot of patience and time to get them to trust him. Now Christy all but followed him around and Stevie was far less sullen. He had stopped throwing his fists around when he got angry, which was something. But at thirteen, he was going to be a bit of a terror for a while anyway.

They were good kids, and they didn't deserve it. Why did kids think it was okay to go after a child because of what their parents did? Mark would never understand the mentality of some people.

As far as he was concerned, that school could use one.

Stevie was staring out the window. He was still scowling, but there was a flicker. He was acknowledging that something worse could have happened. For all of his bravado, he was still a kid. And he didn't need to have such bravado.

Mark sighed.

"I know you hate school, but you do need to get an education. Look, there's another middle school close by attached to the high school. I know the principal and a few of the teachers. They're good people. I can see about getting you in there, if you like."

"I don't know." Stevie narrowed his eyes at Mark. "Why should I go there?"

"It's my old school. I like to think I turned out okay from there."

"No comment."

Mark turned the car into their street. "Seriously, I'll let you think about it for the weekend. If you want to move schools, just let me know and I'll get it sorted. You shouldn't be targeted because of what your parents did."

Stevie snorted.

"No shit."

"Language."

"Compared to what my parents said, that's nothing." Stevie shook his head. "Why are kids so cruel?"

"I've never quite figured that out, and I work with them."

Mark had been in his job for several years, and he still had no idea why some children behaved the way they did. Some of them had bad parents and an awful upbringing, so it was barely a surprise that they had some issues, but then there were those who had a great upbringing but ended up being awful shits anyway. Mark struggled with why a kid who had almost everything going for them would screw it up by becoming a future Michael Myers.

And he had come face to face with someone who said they were Michael Myers' protege. A good kid, barely ten and did well at school with loving parents, who had been watching horror movies in secret when his parents were asleep. They filled his head until he threatened his older sister with a knife. Mark hadn't been able to watch 'Halloween' after that.

Mark pulled his car into the drive of his house. He hadn't planned on leaving work early to deal with a suspension, but his boss understood. Being a foster parent was always going to be tough, but Mark liked to think his work helped him know what children wanted. He wanted to give back what he could. From the look of it, Stevie and Christy were doing well enough.

At least, they hadn't died yet.

His cell phone started ringing in the handheld console. It was work. Sighing, Mark brought out his house keys and handed them to Stevie.

"I've got to take this so you go on inside. And you're not getting on the game system."

"Mark..." Stevie protested.

"You were suspended, and that video game is not a punishment device."

"Depends on what I'm playing." Stevie muttered as he climbed out.

Mark rolled his eyes and answered his phone. He would deal with that later. Right now, his boss needed him.

"Hey, Kat."

"Hey. How's Stevie doing? Is he okay?"

"He'll live. Kids at that school are just horrible." Mark didn't mention the knife. He didn't want to be left cold over that again. "Doesn't help they all know what happened to his parents."

Knowing that his father was a serial killer and his mother had been complicit in getting the victims for him was bad enough. Having other kids reminding him and beating the crap out of him because they consider him a loser just made things worse.

At least Kat understood. She was a foster parent herself, and she threw her heart and soul into protecting all those kids. She was a Mama Bear of the highest order.

"You need anything, Mark, you let me know. I'm sure I can swing a few things."

"I've got it covered for now, but I'll keep it in mind." Mark fought back a yawn. God, he was worn out. "What's up?"

"The Swarbrick-Banfield case has just had its first hearing. Judge Harvey called me a short while ago with information about Ms. Banfield's family."

For a moment, Mark couldn't remember. Then it came to him. Joe Swarbrick was going for an initial custody hearing because his ex-wife Tracey Banfield suddenly decided she wanted her kids after abandoning them. Mark couldn't count how many times he had been to Joe's place and the claims of abuse and neglect were false. Tracey was out for blood. Her attitude had deteriorated over the last couple of years, and Mark was beginning to suspect drug abuse. It didn't fit well.

"I take it her brother Lucas came up in the hearing. Regarding his current status?"

"Yeah, it did." Kat sounded grim. "Judge Harvey was vaguely aware of Lucas Banfield's status as a child molester on parole, but he was shocked when Swarbrick said his ex-wife had been bringing her children to see her brother. Did you know about that?"

Mark blinked.

"No. I didn't. Joe told me about his suspicions, and I spoke to Ms. Banfield, but she said that she wouldn't do that to her kids. She was actually doing it?"

"Yep. You didn't follow it up?"

"I tried, but the family wouldn't let me into the house to do an assessment, and I couldn't get an appointment with any of them." Mark felt like Kat was laying him down for twenty lashes. "I said that I could come back with a sheriff's deputy in the next couple of days if they wouldn't comply. This was actually admitted in court?"

"Sure was. Judge Harvey is still stunned that it was readily admitted to him." Kat's tone hardened. "I want you to class this as a high priority, Mark."

Mark couldn't believe what he was hearing. He knew about the conviction but in spite of the fact he hadn't been able to get an appointment to sit down with Lucas Banfield or his mother Denise, he had been assured that Banfield wasn't anywhere near Lily and James Swarbrick. He had been lied to, and now Mark felt sick. And angry. He always followed things up. Why not now?

"How does she think admitting something like that in court is going to make things okay?"

"She wasn't about to lie to a judge, Mark. She can lie to us, but not them."

"Even so, Tracey Banfield has been behaving very erratically lately. I wouldn't be surprised if she's as crazy as her mother about the conviction."

Mark had seen the paperwork and it made him cold. Lucas Banfield had been married with his own children when he was arrested. Now his ex-wife and three daughters were in another state, having completely vanished. CPS had managed to get word that they were okay and safe, and his colleagues had made a promise not to pass anything on. So far, they had kept their word. Those daughters were all in high school now, and they hadn't seen their dad since they were toddlers. In Mark's opinion, he had been let out way too early. Even with parole, he was dangerous.

"There was physical proof, testimony and witness statements about his actions." Mark rubbed a hand over his face. He was starting to get a headache. "What's there to ignore?"

"You can't get into minds like that, Mark." Kat sighed. "But seeing as you're the one on that shitload, I thought I'd let you know now instead of coming into the office. You're going to need to head over to his parole officer. Chances are he has no idea."

"Why don't you call him? The offices are right next door."

Mark was sure there was a grin on Kat's face as she answered.

"Because there's a particular chocolate hunk who's Banfield's PO, and I thought you might like to...have a chance to interact with him again."

Mark groaned.

"I should never be around you when I'm getting drunk."

Kat laughed.

"Well, you might as well go and look at some eye-candy. And come out red in the face, as always."

"Why don't you go? You drool over him as well."

"Because my husband wouldn't be too impressed. And I don't think Jack would prefer seeing me over you."

She hung up. Mark ended the call at his side and shifted in his seat. Damn, every mention of parole officer Jack McGuire made him as hard as a rock, and Kat knew it. Mark had thought his crush on the guy who worked out of the building next door to the CPS offices wasn't well-known. Jack certainly didn't know,

11

and he was a very observant man. But Kat had seen it, and now Mark had to deal with his supervisor giving him a wink and waggled eyebrows whenever he and Jack were in the same place.

He would be the one who was keeping an eye on Banfield. Just his luck. Mark had been aware that Banfield had a parole officer, but one of his colleagues had gone to speak to Jack. If Mark had known, he would have made the effort.

***

"This is not fucking fair!" The fair-haired man shot to his feet and kicked his chair, knocking it over enough to spin before landing again. "Fuck!"

Jack sighed. He was used to the tantrums when a convict was discovered to be breaking the rules, but it didn't make things any easier. It always gave him a headache.

"Richards, you need to stop shouting and swearing. It's not going to help you."

"Screw you, McGuire." Richards snarled. He began pacing, throwing his hands everywhere. "Why can't I see my children? They're my kids!"

"There is a permanent restraining order against you for them and the rest of your family. Also, you know the conditions of your parole. No attempt to contact them at all."

That was something else that sadly came with parolees looking to enter society again if they could follow the rules. The majority of families, usually former spouses and children, would ask for restraining orders as they were in fear of their lives from someone they once loved. In Max Richards' case, it was very justified; he had been a violent man and almost beat his wife to a pulp because she stayed out with the children longer than she said she would be out. They were better far away from Richards, and Jack wasn't about to change that.

"I'm not going to hurt my kids!" Richard was still shouting. "I love them!"

Jack took a moment to gather himself. God, why did domestic abusers always get to him?

"It's on record that you physically abused all of your children, not to mention the fact they witnessed you almost kill your ex-wife. You were a threat to their safety."

"I never..."

"When you were put on parole, far too early, in my opinion, you agreed to all of these conditions for your parole to happen. And you know what happens if you mess up."

How was it men and women on parole had no idea if they didn't follow their conditions they would be back in jail? It was like they didn't think it would actually happen. In Jack's case, it definitely would.

Richards growled and kicked the fallen chair, sending it across the room.

"What's to stop me seeing them after my parole's up?" He demanded, turning to Jack with a slight smirk. "What's to stop me from seeing my family? Nothing."

Jack rose to his feet. That was when Richards faltered. They were close to the same age and both pretty fit. However, Richards was just brushing six feet. Jack was six feet and easily towered over everyone else. Anyone was about to falter when they saw his long, broad body unfolding itself from his chair. It was why Jack barely stood when he was with a parolee unless he absolutely had to; he liked to intimidate if possible. No convict was going to get one over on him.

"How about the permanent RO they have against you?" Jack folded his arms. "You'll be back in jail so fast your head will be spinning. After your experience in jail previously, you don't want to go back, do you?"

"Fuck, no!"

"Well, you will."

It took a moment for Richards to realize what he had said. His eyes widened.

"But...I never got near them!"

"But you attempted to contact them with a letter to your former in-law's house. You can't do that, and you said you understood."

"Not even a letter?"

"Not even that, and I've read what was in the letter. It's a good thing it didn't get sent." Jack was chilled that he had read the letter. It was not something a father would send to his kids. It was certainly not loving. "As far as they're concerned, you don't exist. You violated your parole, so you're going back to jail."

Richards bared his teeth. Even after seeing that Jack could easily swat him away with one hand, his bravado was still there.

"You can't make me." He sneered.

"Can't I?" Jack picked up his cuffs from beside his keyboard and stepped around the desk. "Turn around, hands behind your back."

"No! I didn't contact them! And they're my kids!" Richards tried to pull away as Jack grabbed him and neatly spun him around. He jabbed an elbow back, almost catching Jack in the ribs. "Fuck off, you bastard! Why would you keep a family separate? I never did anything to them!"

"You're trying to tell me that after all the evidence and the plea deal you took?" Jack had the cuffs on Richards before the other man realized what had happened. "Nice try. You violated what you agreed to, so back into jail you go, and this time you'll serve out the rest of your sentence."

"Fuck you!"

Richards kicked back, catching Jack just below the knee. Jack felt his leg buckle and went down, dragging Richards with him. They hit the floor, and Jack yanked a little more on Richards to make him slam into the carpet a little harder. Richards yowled.

"You bastard! You've busted my elbow!"

"Shut up, you're fine." Jack struggled up and shoved Richards onto his front. "Don't even think about getting up."

He barely looked around as the door opened and his partner came hurrying in.

"Jack, you okay?"

"I'm fine, Josie." Jack gestured at Richards, who was wriggling and snarling on the floor like a pinned snake. "Richards here didn't like the idea of following the rules. Would you call the precinct and ask them to send a car? In the meantime, put him into our holding cell."

"Sure thing." Josie reached down and yanked Richards up by the cuffs. "Come on, you."

15

Richards whined and yowled as he was brought to his feet before being frog marched out of the room. It always amused Jack that Josie, a five-foot-nothing redhead who looked like she was a hundred pounds soaking wet could have a man on their knees unable to get up just by twisting their wrist. It was a sight to see, certainly.

His knee was throbbing as Jack slowly pushed himself to his feet. Richards had missed kicking his knee backwards, but he had still caught just under the patella. Jack balanced on one foot as he bent and straightened his leg. Sore, but it wasn't going to cause him any problems for now. Not unless he had to go sprinting after someone. Jack preferred to avoid that as much as he could.

"Nice to see things are as lively as always in here."

Jack wobbled and spun around. Mark was leaning against the doorframe, hands in his pockets as he watched Jack with a slight smile. He hadn't even heard him come in. His mouth dry, Jack managed to clear his throat.

"Mark. I... What are you doing here?"

"I needed to talk to you." Mark's smile faded. "It's important. Is now a good time?"

"More than good."

For Mark, Jack would happily give him any time if possible. Just the sight of the six-foot, dark-haired CPS worker who always seemed to have a glint in his eye and a smile on that handsome mouth. He had shaven recently, having sported a goatee beard for the last six months. Now he was clean-shaven. Jack liked that look on him.

16

When Mark had first walked into his office regarding one of his parolees, Jack was sure he had been punched in the gut. Mark Washington was just...wow. That was all he could say in the beginning. Jack had been drawn to him immediately. Pretty much anyone who came into contact with him was drawn to him; Mark just had that magnetism. Jack had certainly seen women drooling over him, Josie included. But he barely gave them any thought.

When they were in the same room, it might as well have just been the two of them. Jack barely paid anyone else any attention. Damn, his crush on Mark was embarrassing. At least nobody seemed to have noticed yet.

Remembering where they were, Jack picked up the chair from across the room and set it upright. Mark gave it a bemused look.

"What did the chair ever do to you?"

"Richards didn't like it being in the way. I prefer it was my furniture he kicked instead of his wife, though." Jack went around his desk and sat down. He was a little relieved now there was a physical barrier between them. It would certainly hide the erection he was now starting to sport. "So, what's this about?"

Mark settled into the chair across from him and stretched his legs before sitting forward. His jovial appearance had stopped and now he didn't look happy. If anything, he looked troubled.

"It's about Lucas Banfield."

Jack frowned.

"Lucas Banfield? He's following his conditions. His mother's been very accommodating in making sure her son gets to his appointments on time. And he's never failed a drug test."

"Well, that's about to change." Mark rubbed his hands over his face. "You know that his sister is currently fighting the custody of her kids in court?"

"I do. Lucas has been talking about how he's concerned that his ex-brother-in-law is abusing them. That he wishes there was something he could do."

"And you believed him?"

Jack shook his head.

"I believed you. I met Mr. Swarbrick when I went to let him know about his brother-in-law. He didn't strike me as the type who would abuse his kids. His ex-wife's family, on the other hand..." He shrugged. "They're a different matter."

"And they've been accommodating, have they?"

"Yes. Why?"

Mark took a deep breath.

"Ms. Banfield admitted in court when she was confronted that she had allowed her children to be in her brother's presence since he got out of jail."

"What?"

Jack thought he must have heard wrong. Banfield had been to his office every week and promised that he hadn't been around children. His mother even said they had to move him into her place because of his close proximity to a playground. And they were doing the right things. That was what Jack had been told.

Why did he trust them?

"But...you're from CPS. Wouldn't you have investigated this?"

"I tried. God knows how many times I tried. But they pretended not to be in and refused to meet me at a neutral location or even my office. Said that they had nothing to hide, but still wouldn't come and see me." Mark scowled. "I was planning on going later this week with a deputy to get myself in, but now it's been confirmed out of Ms. Banfield's mouth, it's your territory now."

Jack felt like a fool. He hadn't believed Banfield's declarations of innocence, but he had believed him when they all said he wasn't seeing any children. If he was seeing his niece and nephew when that was expressly forbidden, how many other children was he seeing without his knowledge? And Jack thought he was on top of it all. He liked to think he was keeping his parolees on track.

Clearly not. And he found child molesters to be the worst offenders. They just wouldn't stop. Something in their brain said it didn't apply to them, and Jack had a hard time getting it through their thick skulls, if it got there at all.

"Shit." He had screwed up. He knew it. Jack rubbed his hands over his face. "Do you think he...?"

"I don't know. Joe's kids have said nothing about it, so my gut says no right now. But the fact Banfield is around them at all is enough for me to be concerned. Especially when Ms. Banfield knows about it and still leaves her children in his presence while she wanders off to do fuck knows what."

How the hell did supposedly rational people think it was okay to bend the rules because it was someone they loved? Jack had never figured it out. He found himself standing and pacing. Even with his knee throbbing to the point that Jack had to limp, he paced.

"Lucas Banfield knows that he's not to be in contact with any children at all. He looked like he was going the right way about it. His mother promised that she was keeping him away from kids."

"Well, they clearly ignored what they were supposed to do."

Clearly. Jack had thought Denise Banfield was a little overprotective and hovered around her son like he was six years old, but she had been adamant in that her son would follow the conditions of his parole. How had she missed this, seeing as she was watching Banfield like a hawk? Jack didn't like the idea of a woman in her fifties being complicit to a child molester.

"I'll go and talk to them."

"Good luck with that. I couldn't get to see them at all."

"They wouldn't do that with me. They know if they block me, I can take Banfield back to jail." Jack began to gather his things, getting his gun out of the top draw and clipping the holster to his waistband. "Apparently, they don't think a CPS worker is in the same category as a parole officer."

"I can raise all sorts of shit for them as well."

Jack grinned.

"I'm sure you can. They don't see it that way, though. You'll probably get the spiel that you should be looking at the ex-son-in-law instead of them."

Mark rolled his eyes.

"I've been getting that each and every time. Joe's file has been flagged as one to not open again as all the claims were unfounded and my boss is in the process of getting things together to have Tracey Banfield arrested for filing false reports."

"She won't get much from that."

"Maybe not, but it should be enough for her to stop."

Jack grunted, finding a spare pair of cuffs in his drawer and shoving them into his back pocket. Then he picked up his wallet and keys.

"Knowing my experience with people who do petty things like this, it's going to take something incredibly drastic to get them to stop."

"Especially if they think they're being sneaky about it."

"I won't argue with that. But in my job, there are no second chances. You scrub up or go back to jail." Jack rubbed at his eyes. "Most of these guys can do as they're told because they want to get back to what is normal, but then there are those guys who you shouldn't be anywhere close to. In spite of his behavior lately, Lucas Banfield is one of them."

The guy had been out for eighteen months now, and Jack thought they were getting somewhere. Just another more eighteen months and Banfield would have finished his parole conditions. He would be okay after that, apart from still not being allowed near children. The guy just needed to keep his head down, and if he wanted his freedom, he should have done something about it instead of hiding away the things that would get him arrested again.

Then again, some convicts were just stupid.

"His sister is still allowing him to see her kids when she knows he's not allowed around them. That's what I can't get my head around." Mark ran his hands through his hair with a heavy sigh. "It's like she wants him to go back to jail."

"To me, it sounds like they don't think the rules apply to them." Jack checked his cell phone. "I'll go over there now. You want to come?"

"Best not." Mark rose to his feet. "I asked my neighbor to keep an eye on Stevie for the moment. I don't want to take too long."

"Stevie's home?" Jack looked at the clock. It was nowhere near the time for kids to get out of school. "He's been fighting again, has he?"

"More like he's been getting beaten up again." Mark shook his head. "His parents were the awful ones, and yet he's bullied due to the association. He never did anything wrong."

"Mentality doesn't often work as well as we want it to. It gets twisted at some point."

Mark grunted.

"You got that right. You'll let me know what happens?"

"Of course."

They stared at each other for a moment. Then Mark turned and walked towards the door, closing it behind him. It was then Jack was able to breathe a little more clearly. Damn, Mark Washington could make him feel all warm in some parts of his body and very hard in others. It was going to take him a moment to get his senses back.

Jack had experienced attraction like this before with his wife. Back then, he had been confident enough to act upon it. But with Mark, it was two years on and Jack couldn't bring the courage to say anything.

You're such a wimp, Jack. A wimp.

Chapter Two

Denise Banfield lived in Encino, just off the Encino Reservoir. Jack had been to their house previously and had been very impressed by it. Her husband's family had been very wealthy people and Denise was very successful in her job. When her husband passed away ten years before, he left pretty much everything to his wife and kids. And it showed with their home. Jack had no idea how many extra renovations had been done on the place, but it was easily the nicest house on the street.

Better than his comfy but much smaller apartment, certainly. This house did look like a good place to have a family in. Just like Mark's house. He and the children lived in a nice part of Winnetka. Jack had been over several times, and he was impressed. For a bachelor with two pre-teen children, he certainly knew how to keep the place clean. And he was very strict on making sure the kids ate healthily and they had clean clothes all the time. Jack had never seen a single parent that well put together.

Jack felt a slight pang in his chest as he thought about that. A family. His parents were always pestering him to find someone and have children. His wife Tessa hadn't been able to have children, and Jack was okay with that. When she died from cancer, Jack had been devastated. He couldn't even think about having a family after losing the woman he loved. It had resulted in cutting contact with his mother for nearly a year because all she would do was pester him about giving her grandbabies. She finally understood that she needed to back off.

They weren't getting any younger. And Jack would like to oblige - he loved kids - but he hadn't found the right person.

Maybe he should do what Mark had done. Register to be a foster parent so he could help out kids on a semi-permanent basis. But then his job was dangerous and that might work against him. Jack didn't want to bring his work home where there were children, and some of his disgruntled employees had been known to follow him home to harass him.

Perhaps that wasn't such a good idea.

Jack pushed the thought of kids out of his head and pulled into the driveway of Denise's house. Her car was still there, as was the car she let her son drive. At least both of them were home. Although that would make the conversation a little tense if Denise were hanging around; she tended to try and speak for her son.

Jack had looked up enmeshment when Josie had told him about it. These two would be a picture next to the definition.

Denise answered the door once Jack rang the bell. She was one of those few women who didn't need to crane her head back to look at him. Denise Banfield was easily six-three, as tall as her son, and built like an Olympic athlete. She did look good for fifty-eight, Jack had to admit, her black hair cropped into a pixie cut and her makeup delicately applied.

She looked harmless enough, but Jack's previous interactions said she was like a coiled snake waiting to strike if someone said a bad thing about her children, especially her son. Now she was looking up at Jack was slightly bewildered look, which turned into a bright smile.

"Mr. McGuire. I wasn't aware we were having a visit today."

"I am entitled to do inspections without warning, Mrs. Banfield. It's part of the parole conditions." Jack glanced into the house. "Can I come in? I need to speak to your son."

"Of course." Denise stepped aside. "Lucas is out on the patio. We're about to get the barbecue out."

Jack's stomach growled. He loved a good barbecue. Mark was pretty good with the grill as well. On good days, they would always be out there doing the grilling.

Not now! You're on duty, you idiot!

Jack followed Denise through the house and onto the patio. Lucas was there, laying out the burgers on the grill. He was a huge solid hulk of a man wearing a pale lilac apron. Jack couldn't help but smile at the sight of a thirty-five-year-old man almost as tall as him and built like a weightlifter wearing a frilly apron.

"Looks good on you, Banfield."

"Oh, Mr. McGuire." Lucas' face darkened as he fumbled to take the apron off. "I wasn't expecting you. Mom and I were just about to have a late lunch."

"So I noticed." Jack stepped aside as Lucas went into the kitchen. He waited until Lucas had washed his hands. "I've got some disturbing news, Lucas. And I need to hear it from you. This will affect your parole."

"That sounds ominous." Lucas dried his hands. "What's up?"

"It's probably that bastard Swarbrick again." Denise said with a scowl. She folded her arms and pouted. "He's always saying things against my family. Did it during their hearing today. Tried to drag our name through the mud. Tracey's furious."

Jack could imagine. He was furious that this had been admitted in court and he hadn't been made aware of it. And it was like the Banfields hadn't clicked.

"You think she should be given full custody?" He asked. "Even though it's clear that she's not in the right stable condition to have them? She's been very erratic and her outbursts were concerning."

Denise smarted, her lips pressing tightly together.

"My daughter is of sound mind, Mr. McGuire. She's a good mother."

"If she was a good mother, Mrs. Banfield, then she wouldn't be leaving her children here with you when her brother is in the house." Jack turned to Lucas. "Especially when she's more than aware that he's not allowed around children at all."

"So what?" Lucas shrugged. "I was never left alone with them."

That threw Jack a little. He was half-expecting them to deny, as they had done before. The two of them said they wouldn't allow Lily and James to come in at all, and that Denise would see her grandkids elsewhere. He stared at them.

"Are you actually telling me that you were in contact with Lily and James Swarbrick? In this house?"

"He was in the same room as them, Mr. McGuire." Denise corrected. "He was never in actual contact. And he was never left alone with my grandbabies. I was always here."

Jack felt sick. He'd had child molesters try to skate around the rules before, but this was different. In a way, he was connected to it all. He had listened to Mark talk about this case, and he had met Joe Swarbrick. The ex-husband was angry that his children were in contact with his former in-laws, but he loved his children. He was much shorter and not as heavy as Lucas, but Jack could see Joe ripping his ex-brother-in-law to pieces if he could get his hands on the guy.

Jack would have done the same in his position. But he had to put that aside. He took a deep breath.

"I speak to you every week, Banfield, and you tell me that you're never alone with children."

"Right. I'm never alone."

Jack growled.

"You know you're not supposed to be around children at all. After not telling me about this, how do I know you're not putting your hands on children now?"

"He's never touched Lily and James!" Denise protested. "He loves them!"

"He said he loved the kids he touched as well. You think I'm going to believe that?"

Denise floundered. Lucas was wavering a little, a flicker of worry behind his eyes. Good. He needed to know that he had screwed up big-time.

"Lucas has got a right to see his niece and nephew." Denise said stoutly. "And they love seeing him. Lily and James adore their Uncle Lucas."

"I don't care that two children love their uncle. You two seem to be ignoring the fact he's not allowed around children. Not in the same room. You knew that."

"I can't help it if I want to see my babies."

Her babies? Jack hated it when grandmothers called their grandchildren their babies. Made it sound rather icky.

"You could do that elsewhere. Anywhere that wasn't here or make Banfield leave for a period of time. He's supposed to have a job, isn't he?"

"I can't get a job right now." Lucas said sullenly. "My last job fired me for no reason, and I can't seem to get past the interview stage."

Jack called bullshit on that. Lucas had always been slack on working. He had been like that before he got arrested. Why change now? He made a mental note to call Lucas' employer. Why the hell hadn't they called him?

"I can't tell Tracey to drop them off elsewhere." Denise was still protesting. "I can't say no if my grandbabies want to see my son."

"From what I've heard, Tracey is leaving them here for hours on end, sometimes the whole weekend." Jack scowled. "You didn't think to tell her that maybe she should look after her own children on the weekends she's got them?"

"Tracey likes to go out and have fun."

"Then she should do it when she doesn't have children around, not push them on you. Even if she wasn't helping violate her brother's parole, it doesn't look good in getting custody."

"Their father fills those kids' heads with a lot of things." Lucas snapped. "He's the bad one here, not us. Why aren't you bothering him?"

"Because he's not on parole for felony crimes." Jack shot back. He felt like he had stepped into an alternate reality. "I can't believe you just said that,

29

Lucas! You went to prison for molestation crimes. You were lucky you didn't serve the whole term, and it was harsh. You got a chance to get out early and you're screwing it up because you three believe it's okay you can see your niece and nephew as long as you're not alone? That's not how it works!"

"He never touched them!" Denise cried. She hurried to put herself between Jack and Lucas, giving Jack a pleading look. "He's a good boy, Mr. McGuire. And he never hurt those children. They were all liars!"

Jack silently counted to ten. How they couldn't see this as wrong, he had no idea. It made him feel sick.

"Trust me, Mrs. Banfield, I know who the liar was. Just like you've been lying to me all this time."

"I never touched Lily and James!" Lucas shouted.

"Doesn't matter. You were in contact with them and that violates your parole? How long would you have done this? All the way until I cleared you to come out of your probationary period? If Mr. Swarbrick and his attorney hadn't brought it to Judge Harvey's attention, then we wouldn't have known." He reached into his pocket and drew out his cuffs. "You're going back to jail, Lucas. Turn around and put your hands behind your back."

For a moment, Lucas was frozen. Then he darted to the counter and withdrew a knife from the knife block. He brandished it at Jack.

"Not a chance am I going back."

Denise was staring at her son like he had gone mad. Jack couldn't believe what he was seeing. At least it was a knife and the bastard hadn't charged at him. That would have sent him flying.

"You're kidding me, right?" Jack withdrew his gun and pointed it at Lucas' head. "You do know I can shoot you before you touch me."

"I'm not going back to jail!"

"If you didn't want to go back, you shouldn't have been a fucking idiot. Now drop the knife."

"Please, don't!" Denise cried. She looked like she was about to cry as she tried to grab his arm. "Don't shoot him! He's a good boy!"

Jack growled and shrugged her off.

"You touch me again, Mrs. Banfield, and I'll arrest you, too. You've been complicit in this, and that won't go unnoticed when I make the parole board aware." Stepping away from Denise as she reached for him again, Jack focused on Lucas. "Turn around, Banfield."

"You turn around."

"I'll put a bullet in your head and I'll be completely justified." Jack was bluffing there, although he was sure he wouldn't be penalized too much. "Do you want to walk out of here or be carried out? Either way is fine with me, but if you're going to threaten me with a knife I'll shoot you."

Denise wailed loudly. It was a little weird seeing a middle-aged woman sobbing in such a dramatic fashion. Jack ignored her. If he shifted his attention, Lucas could go for him. And Jack wasn't interested in having a knife coming at him.

Then Lucas lunged. He went for Jack's gut. Jack stepped to the side and slammed his gun onto Lucas'

31

arm. Lucas cried out and his arm spasmed. He dropped the knife. Then Jack grabbed Lucas' wrist and twisted it around, causing Lucas to be knocked off his feet and landing hard on the floor. Lucas lay dazed as Jack pushed him onto his front and holstered his gun before he started to snap the cuffs on. He was armed and could have shot Lucas, since he thought he could hurt him.

"Did you seriously need to do that, Lucas? Seriously?"

"Let him go!" Denise started towards him. "He did nothing wrong!"

"Like I said, Mrs. Banfield, you touch me and I'm arresting you as well." Jack brought out his cell phone, Lucas moaning underneath him. "I'm going to call for backup. If you even attempt to block any of us from doing our job, you'll be joining your son."

Denise's bottom lip quivered, but she didn't say anything. Instead, she screamed and stormed into the other room, slamming doors behind her. Jack was half-hoping she would attack him so he could arrest her; she was far too unstable for his liking.

Considering who she had for children, it wasn't a surprise.

✳✳✳

"Mark?"

Mark looked up. Stevie was in the doorway to his office, shuffling from foot to foot as he fiddled with the sleeve of his hoodie. Mark put his pen down and turned.

"Yeah, buddy? What's up?"

Stevie shoved his hands in his pockets, and shuffled into the room. His head was bowed, not willing to look at him. Mark knew the look. It was what Stevie did when he was about to accept a punishment. His parents used to beat him, and Mark had vowed that no adult would ever lay a hand on him again. Even though Stevie knew that Mark would never hurt him, he still flinched whenever he had done something wrong. That broke Mark's heart. The kid didn't need that.

"I…" Stevie took a deep breath and looked up. "I'm sorry."

"What are you sorry about?"

"For getting into another fight. For being an embarrassment." Stevie swallowed. "For being a screw-up."

He looked close to tears. He was a teenager and looked like a shaking little boy. Mark swallowed the lump in his throat and beckoned Stevie over, opening his arms. Stevie went to him and hugged him tightly, burying his face into Mark's neck. Even a year after finally getting Stevie to be okay with touching, this made Mark happy. Stevie was a tough kid, and he tried to show himself as one. But he just wanted to be loved and accepted.

"Look at me, Stevie." Mark eased the boy back and clasped his shoulders, giving the kid a smile. "You're not a screw-up. Far from it. And you didn't embarrass me. You scared me, certainly, when I found out about the knife, but I wasn't embarrassed. I'm just glad you're okay."

"Okay." Stevie bit his lip. "You're not going to send me away for getting into fights, are you?"

"Why would I do that?"

33

"Dad would have beaten me for fighting."

The mere mention of the man filled Mark with fury. He was a disgusting piece of work. It was a good thing he was in jail for a very long time, because he didn't deserve to be outside in the real world.

"I'm not your dad. And I'm not going to hit you for standing up for yourself."

"Thank you."

"Did you think I was going to send you away?"

"A little bit." Stevie shrugged. "Dad used to threaten me with that when I was naughty."

"You were barely ten."

"He still did it."

No wonder Stevie and Christy never said anything, even though they were always in the house when their father was carrying out his heinous crimes. They were more terrified of what would happen if the toxic family broke apart. It should never be like that, not for any children. Stevie and Christy were good kids, and it had taken a lot of time and patience to get them to how they should be as children. Mark wasn't about to send them away and have that gone. He wouldn't want to send either child away, anyway. He loved them too much.

"Thank you." Stevie squared his shoulders. "Can you see about me going to your school soon? I think it will be better for me to have a change of scenery."

Mark smiled.

"Of course. I'll give the principal a call."

He had actually given the man a call on the way back from Jack's office to ask for his advice. Principal Dockerty had offered to get Stevie settled in at his middle school first thing Monday morning and all Mark needed to do was to get Stevie to turn up, but Mark decided to delay taking the offer. It was Stevie's choice, after all. Mark wanted him out of his old place, but he didn't want to force Stevie anything. Now he could call his old principal and ask if the offer was still open for when Stevie had finished his week's suspension. The guy had made sure Mark didn't screw up as a kid, so he could easily do it for Mark's foster kid.

A blonde-haired girl almost as tall as Stevie poked her head around the door.

"Mark, Mr. McGuire's at the door."

Mark's pulse jumped. Jack was already here? He wasn't expecting to see him tonight. He gulped and dusted down his shirt.

"I'll be a moment. Have you let him in?"

"He's in the kitchen."

"Thanks, Christy."

Christy nodded and disappeared. Stevie gave Mark a smile and hugged him again.

"Thanks, Mark."

"It's okay, buddy." Mark glanced at the clock. "I'll order food shortly. Do you have any homework to do?"

Stevie groaned.

"I still have to do that?"

"Don't slack just yet. Besides," Mark winked, "you get it done, I'll give you an extra hour on the video games tomorrow when your ban is up."

Stevie's eyes widened. Then he grinned before disappearing. He would do anything to get onto that new console system. Mark felt that getting it was worth it to see Stevie's eyes light up. The kid was such a big gamer. It certainly made him happy.

But sitting here wasn't going to make Mark happy. And there was a hunk in his kitchen. Standing up, Mark dusted himself down, almost checking his hair before realizing that he was being an idiot. He shouldn't be doing that. Jack had seen him at his worst, practically, so why bother?

He couldn't help but check himself in the mirror on the way to the kitchen. He was now in jeans and shirt instead of his suit, and the jeans were brand new, still relatively stiff. If he ended up showing how aroused he was, Jack would be able to tell. And Jack wasn't about to do that in front of his kids; they didn't need to see that.

Jack was in the kitchen, leaning on the center counter talking to Christy. He had changed into jeans and a dark gray t-shirt that hugged his body. It was almost like he had had the t-shirt sprayed on. Christy was giggling at something Jack had said, twirling her hair around her fingers. Mark had to fight back a smile. Christy was taken with Jack as well. Who wouldn't when he used that gorgeous smile? Anyone would be melting. Mark certainly did, and Christy adored him.

Jack looked up as Mark stepped into the room, his eyes looking Mark up and down in open appreciation.

"Hey."

"Hey." God, why did he have to sound so breathless. Mark cleared his throat and glanced at

Christy. "Can you give us a moment, Christy? We need to discuss something about work."

"Okay." Christy pouted, clearly not happy. "Is Mr. McGuire staying for dinner?"

"I don't know." Jack gave Mark a smile. "If Mark says it's okay..."

How could he deny him anything with that smile?

"I'm only getting takeout."

Jack chuckled.

"Then I might just say yes."

Christy brightened. She pushed off the counter and headed towards the door. Mark ruffled her hair on the way past.

"Hey!"

"Go and start on your homework and I might let you play that game I got you after dinner. Stevie won't be hogging the console."

Christy grinned and hurried towards the stairs. Jack laughed.

"Are you always bribing them with video games?"

"It's just an incentive. And you haven't seen how awesome the new gaming console is."

"I don't do video games. I haven't got the time."

"Neither did I, until I got children." Mark shut the door and moved towards the counter. "How did it go with Banfield?"

Jack sighed.

"Not good. They admitted to it. I had Banfield arrested after he went for me with a knife."

"He what?"

"Didn't get anywhere near me. He's going to be having a sore wrist, though."

Shit. Mark hadn't thought it could get that dangerous. He pushed aside the panic, forcing himself to calm down. Jack was okay. He wasn't hurt. There was no need to worry.

"You say they actually admitted to it?"

"They did." Jack's expression was grim. "They told me so many times that they weren't around children, but it seems like they weren't adding Lily and James into that equation."

"Sounds like it." Mark shook his head. "I didn't think they would actually do that. And I wasn't expecting Tracey Banfield to readily admit it in court, either, after the accusations towards her ex."

"Neither did I. I remember her when Banfield came out of jail a couple of years back. She seemed rather put together and that she would keep her children safe. Now she looks like she's on something."

"Drugs?"

"Probably. Where she's getting them from, I have no idea, but her erratic behavior has certainly started since her brother went on parole, which tells me he's to blame for it."

Mark wouldn't be surprised. Toxic family members tended to change the dynamics in people just by being present.

"And they didn't think that Banfield being around his niece and nephew when he's banned from doing so was something we needed to be aware of? Even if Tracey was doing it on her own and they were caught on the back foot, they should have said something."

"I think they believe because he was never alone with them it should be okay." Jack leaned his crossed arms on the counter. "Trying to find loopholes."

"That's not a loophole, that's just another way to get into trouble."

"Exactly. Don't think they see it like that."

Mark grunted. God, this was more of a mess than he realized. He pressed his fingers to the bridge of his nose.

"At least Lily and James weren't abused. Joe would have brought it up long before, and they don't behave like kids who have been abused."

"That's the only slight silver lining to all this." Jack grumbled.

Only very slightly. Mark knew people's mentality would go all over the place at times, especially when family were involved. Nobody wanted to believe family could be capable of such awful things. And there was something not quite right with that family. Mark had suspected it with his first interaction with Tracey. He couldn't quite put his finger on it, though.

Whatever it was, Joe did a good thing getting out of that madness.

"They've got another hearing on Monday where Judge Harvey gives the official verdict on the custody arrangement."

"Do you think he's going to give Tracey Banfield what she wants?"

"I hope not. I doubt it." Mark frowned. "Judge Harvey's a good guy. And he makes sure everything he does is in the best interest of the children."

Craig Harvey was an advocate for children. He always had them in mind, and he was the most respected family court judge in Northridge. Other judges had rotated in and out, but Craig had stayed. He said it as his mission to make sure kids had a voice. Mark had to respect that.

His stomach growled, which had Mark grimacing. Damn, he should have ordered food already.

"You really want to stay for dinner? We usually just get pizza or a Chinese."

"Either's fine for me." Jack gave a slight smile and shrugged. "I haven't really got anything to go back for."

Was that his way of saying he was single and available? Mark felt heat tickling the back of his neck. He had often wondered if Jack was single, but he had never openly asked. Mark was aware that Jack had been married before and his wife had died of cancer ten years before, but it wasn't clear if he had anyone else in his life; Jack played things close to his chest when it came to his private life.

Was he trying to tell Mark something? Mark gulped.

"Does it get lonely on your own?"

"Does it for you?"

"I've got two kids running around here. I don't have time to be lonely."

"You know what I mean."

They stared at each other. Was it suddenly a lot warmer in there? Mark could feel the sweat trickling down his back. Damn, Jack could make any situation hot, especially with the way he looked at someone like the way he was looking at Mark.

You are so lucky the kids are in the house, or you would be getting jumped by now.

"It...it can get a bit lonely on occasion. But I make do. What about you?"

"Sometimes." Jack glanced away. "I miss having someone around me. I like the quiet, but it can get suffocating. I guess that's why I'm always at work."

Mark managed a slight grin.

"You need to get yourself a girlfriend. Give you something to do, or someone."

"Or maybe a boyfriend. Not fussed either way."

Mark blinked.

"You bisexual?"

"Pansexual."

"Oh."

That was not quite the response he expected. Mark had never asked about Jack's sexuality, but he did wonder if Jack was bisexual. He had been married to a woman, who had been lovely according to Josie, but from the way Jack looked at Mark he wondered if the door swung both ways. But pansexual?

Mark realized he had been staring with Jack looking at him with a raised eyebrow. God, Mark felt like an idiot.

"Interesting." Now that sounded lame. "I never realized."

"Why would you? We don't look any different to anyone else."

"I guess." Mark managed a smile. "Although it's nice to know you're not fussy."

"If you float my boat, you're in it."

Mark didn't know what to say to that. His mouth opened and closed a few times with Jack giving him a heated look. Did he float Jack's boat? Damn. Maybe he had a chance, after all.

"Mark?"

Mark jumped and spun around. Stevie was in the doorway, giving him a strange look. Mark hadn't realized that the door had opened.

"Yeah, Stevie?"

"Did you say we were having dinner soon? Christy and I are getting hungry."

"Oh. Right." Mark rubbed his hands on his jeans. Suddenly, his hands were sweaty. "Pizza or Chinese?"

"Chinese." Stevie made a face. "I need something to keep me focused. I hate math."

"That your homework right now?"

"Sadly."

Stevie hated math. He was good at his other subjects, but when it came to numbers he couldn't get his head around them. It was like his brain just didn't want to work. Mark understood; he was the same with

42

it. Which was why helping Stevie with his homework was a bit of a nightmare.

"Want some help?" Jack asked. "I'm pretty good at math."

Mark stared at him.

"Are you sure?"

"I'm sure. It would give me something to do while you're ordering food."

"Thanks." Stevie grinned. "I hope you're better at math than Mark is."

Jack laughed and came around the counter.

"I'm sure everyone's better than Mark at math."

"Hey! Why are you ganging up on me?"

Jack was still laughing as he passed Mark and headed towards the dining table. Their arms brushed and Mark felt the shivers go up his arm. He was sure the hairs on his arm were prickling. He watched as Jack and Stevie sat at the table, Stevie laying out his homework from the binder.

"You...what do you fancy for Chinese?"

"Anything as long as it's hot." Jack shot him a glance over his shoulder, his eyes glinting. "I'm sure you can find something that will float my boat."

That sounded far more sexual than it should have been.

Chapter Three

Mark was glad to be heading into work. Sort of. He loved his job, but it did leave him emotionally drained. It was no wonder most of his coworkers left after a couple of years; it just sucked the soul out of the people who worked in CPS. Mark had been there for six years now, and he wouldn't have it any other way. The kids needed someone to be their voice, and Mark was happy to be that for them.

They weren't always bad children. If they were bad, it was often by circumstances. Although the ones who were bad and nothing had happened to warrant it were the scary ones. Mark wished he could help the parents, and there were parents who genuinely wanted to do whatever they could to have CPS sign off on them, and then there were people who believed they were being targeted for a myriad of reasons.

Mark got exhausted doing that all day, but it was worth it. Especially when he got home and saw Stevie and Christy. They were worth doing it all again the next day.

At least it was Stevie's last day in suspension. Mark had already notified the school that due to their inability to stop the harassment by the other students, Stevie was moving schools and Mark was notifying the school board before launching an investigation into the bullying. It was far more rife than Mark realized when Stevie told him. As far as he was aware, the teachers did nothing about it. Stevie would be in a new school and in a better place; Principal Dockerty would not tolerate bullying at all.

Thankfully, Christy's school was a little nicer. Not completely, but she wasn't being bullied. That would change once she got to middle school in the next year, Mark was sure. Christy was tough, but she wouldn't be able to withstand what Stevie had gone through. Girls were far nastier than boys, Mark had found out. They could smile sweetly to your face while stabbing you in the back. The girls Mark had gone to school with had been very good at it.

The only upside was that Stevie had something to do. Jack had offered to pay Stevie to do some odd jobs for him. He took the week off, much to Mark's surprise, and said that Stevie could head over throughout the week to either work on the garden or help Jack out with a few DIY stuff around the house. Mark had tried to protest - he didn't have to do all of that - but Jack was insistent. He said it would keep Stevie busy, and he would keep an eye on the kid.

Mark hadn't known what to say to that, but Stevie had looked delighted at the thought of doing something that wasn't keeping him shut up in the house. And it did mean Mark could go to work and not rely too much on his mother. Amber Washington worked part-time, so she could watch Stevie occasionally, but she did have to work as well and Mark wasn't comfortable leaving Stevie alone in the house all day. Last time he did that, Stevie had made a mess that Mark didn't think was possible to make in such a short space of time. It was time he learned more about responsibility.

And Amber lived two streets over from Jack, so Mark could drop Stevie off at Amber's and he could walk over to Jack's when he had had his breakfast. Amber was happy to be a taxi at the end of the day providing Stevie did the work. Jack would make sure of that.

Mark didn't know why he deserved to have Jack helping him out. But he appreciated it. At least he would be able to come home and not find it looking like a bomb had gone through it.

Mark was whistling as he headed into his offices. There were no face-to-face appointments today, only paperwork. Mark preferred the paperwork side of it, especially when it made his desk look neat and tidy. His colleagues called him odd, but Mark was fine with it. Before Stevie and Christy came along, Mark would be at his desk until close to two in the morning if he wasn't watching the time. Now he was able to organize his time better and get things done. Stevie and Christy were old enough that they could look after themselves for an hour or so if Mark got delayed, but he rarely did that. Having someone at home made getting off his computer a little easier.

Would that work if he had a partner to come home to? More than likely, but it would depend on the partner. Jack? Mark would be running home.

He did wonder what Jack would say if he wanted something more than just friendship. There were some very obvious flirtations now, Jack coming over every day for dinner after bringing Stevie home. Mark was surprised but he didn't stop it, although he wished they could really be alone. Having children close by and with very sharp ears could kill the mood. Mark didn't want to explain that to his foster kids what he was up to. His sexuality was never raised with either of them, neither of them asking. Christy had asked him once why he hadn't got a girlfriend and Mark just said that he was always busy. If they knew he was gay, they hadn't mentioned it.

Might have ended up rather weird for all of them if the kids caught him with Jack in that way.

Mark pushed that aside as he stepped into the elevator. He didn't want to go through all that right now, not when he was heading into work. It wasn't a good idea to get an erection in this suit. And anything involving fantasies about Jack McGuire gave him an erection that was very hard to get rid of. Mark didn't want to frighten his coworkers.

Mark stepped off the elevator and almost ran into a woman pacing the lobby. He started to apologize and step around, only to find the woman clutching his arms.

"Excuse me, I..." Then he saw who was in front of him. "Ms. Banfield. What are you doing here?"

"I need to speak to you, Mr. Washington." Tracey looked rather distraught. "Now."

"I don't have an appointment with you."

"Please, Mark." Tracey's fingers dug into his arms. "I need to talk to you."

She didn't look good. She was dressed in a simple red sweater and jeans, her hair held back by a red headband, all put together, but there was a wild look in her eyes. It was a look Mark had seen many times on addicts. She was high right now, or she was close to coming down from it. Mark was sure she was going to break sooner rather than later.

If she tried to deny she was on drugs now, chances were nobody would believe her. Mark wouldn't believe her. That court order to be drug tested and go into rehab hadn't sunk in.

And she wasn't going to leave anytime soon. Sighing, Mark shrugged his arms away and beckoned her to follow him. The sooner he could get her out of there, the bigger. Tracey could be desperate now, but

47

she had been very combative with her lawyer. Joe had said Tracey was just as horrid to her attorney, enough for them to fire her. That didn't surprise Mark after the way he saw Tracey behave in court on Monday.

They reached Mark's desk, where Mark put down his laptop case. Then he indicated for Tracey to join him. Crossing the huge room that had been divided up into cubicles, they stepped into the empty conference room. Mark closed the door as Tracey paced across the room, her arms wrapped around her waist. She spun around so quickly Mark was surprised she didn't fall over.

"Mom called me. They're going to send Lucas back to jail today."

"I was aware that he was having his parole hearing today." Mark folded his arms. "I'm not surprised they revoked his release."

If they hadn't, they were more stupid than Mark thought. No one in their right mind would let a child molester be around a kid.

"But he'll die in prison." Tracey cried. "He's not strong enough to face prison again."

Mark almost burst out laughing. He had seen the size of Lucas. He looked like he could handle himself easily. It was the other prisoners Mark was worried about if Lucas lost his temper. Apparently, he had one wicked right hook.

"Lucas should've thought about that before he violated his parole. He was told that he couldn't be around children, and yet you kept leaving your children with your mother while he was living there. Were you trying to get him back in jail?"

"I didn't mean anything like it!" Tracey now looked panicked. "Mom said it was okay!"

"And you should've said no. You should've kept your kids while you had custody of them, not try and change the goalposts because you don't like being told no."

Tracey bristled. Mark couldn't keep up with her switch of emotions. It was like she had multiple personalities stacking up to come forward.

"Lucas is my brother. Would you want me to turn my back on my brother?"

"I would've wanted you to follow the rules of his parole so he could be back on the streets. Not being around children still applies even after that, but if you loved him enough you wouldn't do that."

"Family doesn't split apart, Mr. Washington."

Mark snorted.

"Considering that's what you did to your ex-husband and he was meant to be your family, that's a bit of a hypocritical thing to say, isn't it?"

Tracey flushed. Her eyes narrowed.

"Joe never liked Lucas. Said he was a creep. Lucas is not a creep."

She had to be smoking something really strong to believe that Lucas Banfield wasn't a creep. Mark wondered how this woman was rational and a decent person like Joe said she had been when they first met and got married. Living far away from her mother had done Tracey some good, and she had been strong. But as soon as they came back around the same time Lucas got out of jail, it all went to hell.

Lucas had to be the catalyst for Tracey's downward spiral. Mark couldn't see anything else. He was far more dangerous to Tracey than she realized. Jack had thought Lucas had fed Tracey drugs and she only became a decent person and got clean when he wasn't around. Mark was inclined to agree with him.

"Tracey, your brother is a convicted child molester. Four counts of it. You know the conditions of his parole. You were there when they were dictated to Lucas. Ever since he came back out, you've been defending him when before you refused to have anything to do with him."

"I always defended him!"

"Not when you were living several states away. Joe commented that you changed when you guys moved to California. Something else is going on." Mark looked her up and down. "I wonder if I took your socks off, would I find needle tracks?"

"I'm not taking drugs!" Tracey almost screamed.

"The dilation of your pupils says otherwise."

Tracey's nostrils flared. Mark braced himself, half-expecting her to launch herself at him. Then Tracey squared her shoulders and took a deep breath, letting it out slowly.

"Nothing is going on with me. I'm just breaking free of a bad marriage. Or trying to. Now I can't have my babies at all."

"You can have your children more than right now if you do as the judge recommended..."

"No!" Tracey swiped a hand through the air. "That judge is a fool. I don't need to do any of that shit."

50

"You haven't got a choice, it's court-mandated." Mark was beginning to get impatient. "You don't do it, you'll never see your kids again. That's written into your agreement. I'm sure your new attorney has said that as well."

Tracey snorted.

"My new attorney. If my old attorney hadn't switched around so much, I wouldn't need to find a new one."

Mark bit back a retort. He knew the reasons for the changing of lawyers. Alex had ended up having a one-night stand with Joe, and now they were embarking on a relationship. His female colleague had then represented Tracey for her final hearing before firing her as a client. They wouldn't touch her after her antics, and Mark couldn't blame them. From the way Tracey had acted, she was lucky Alex hadn't kicked her beforehand.

He knew the custody agreement. Joe had primary and legal custody and Tracey would get restricted visitation which would be looked at again once she did rehab and parenting classes. They were ordered by the court and Tracey had thirty days to comply. From the way she was acting, that wasn't happening.

"Fine, then." Tracey adjusted her sweater with a sniff. "They'll come and find me when they're eighteen if it's going to be that bad. I know they'll look for me."

"Don't put all your hopes on that. And you shouldn't put all that onto your children's shoulders when you should be straightening yourself out."

"There's nothing to straighten out."

They were going to go around in circles all morning. Mark had no time for that. He took a deep breath.

"You, your brother and your mother did a very bad thing. Now you're suffering the consequences. You want to be a parent? Do what's best for your children and follow what the judge told you to do."

But Tracey shook her head.

"Not a chance. I don't need to do anything. I'm the mother, so I should have custody."

"Doesn't work like that and you know it."

Tracey looked him up and down. Had she expected him to agree with her and promise to do something? She already knew that she was in serious trouble for filing false CPS reports on her ex-husband, so the fact she had shown her face here after that was pretty brazen. Mark's boss had her put on a special list to not take any type of reports due to her being unreliable. Did she really think Mark would be on her side?

Tracey's mouth curled in a sneer. She was all over the place with her emotions again.

"I bet you let Joe off all the time because you're fucking him." Her voice dripped venom. "I only found out yesterday that he was fucking my attorney. Did he do the same to you as well?"

"Now you're crossing a line, Ms. Banfield."

"Did he?"

Mark glared.

"No, he didn't. And if you're going to accuse me of anything further, you're to leave the office immediately." He grabbed at the door handle and yanked the door open. "Now, before I have you thrown out. I can easily call security to escort you down."

Tracey's eyes flashed.

"You're a butt-fucking…"

"Out! Now!"

Mark didn't broadcast his sexuality, and he wasn't interested in having it brandished around the office. Tracey looked him up and down with further sneering. Now she was starting to turn into the person Mark remembered in the courtroom. She looked rather scary.

"We'll get you, Washington." She hissed, almost spitting in his face as she passed him. "You and McGuire ruined us. We'll get you for this."

"You have five seconds to get out of my sight before I report you for threatening behavior. I'm sure that's not going to look good on your own record."

Tracey's eyes narrowed. Then she stalked out of the room, purposely bumping into Mark's shoulder. She went across the office with her nose in the air, a few of the male workers watching her go with slight bemusement. Mark leaned on the doorframe and took a deep breath. So much for having a good day today.

**

Jack was finishing a late breakfast when there was a knock at the front door. Putting his breakfast things on the counter, he crossed the apartment and opened the door. Stevie was on the porch, giving him a bright smile.

"Hey, Jack."

"Hey, Stevie."

Jack looked towards the street and saw Amber Washington's car waiting on the curb. He gave the older woman a smile and a wave, getting a wave in return before Amber pulled away. Jack beckoned Stevie inside.

"You ready to get going on the back yard? We've got a lot to do today."

"I think so." Stevie frowned. "I'm not sure I like gardening."

"I don't know why. You're good at it. Why don't you start on the lavender bush? It's taking over back there."

Stevie grunted. Then he headed through the apartment. It was less an apartment and more of a one-floor house, but it was tiny having been part of a much larger space that had been split into three apartments. Jack took the smallest one as it was just him and he was a simple guy with simple means. The complex he lived in was quiet and his neighbors were decent people, so he didn't have much to complain about.

Having said that, he often ended up being the one who did the gardening in their communal garden out back. The couples in the other two apartments used the gardens, but they had no idea how to maintain it beyond mowing the lawn. And the bushes did get overgrown. One couple were constantly travelling for work and the others had small children, so they were consistently busy. It came down to Jack.

There were times when he didn't mind, but Jack would prefer someone else did the gardening. Or when he had help. It wasn't too much to ask. So, when Mark said Stevie had a week where he would most likely be with his foster grandmother, Jack had suggested Stevie come to help him out. It wasn't fair for Amber to look after Stevie or for Mark to lose time out of work. They doted on the teen, but there was only so much they could do without support. And it was just them.

Jack had enough vacation time saved up to stay home and give him something to do. Once Stevie got himself focused, he was a good worker. He just needed to channel himself properly once he had some responsibility. And Stevie was better at gardening than he said he was.

As Stevie went out the back and into the garden, Jack started putting his breakfast things away. Once he was done, he would check his emails and then go out to help Stevie. It was a warm day despite being nearer to winter than Jack would have liked, so he was going to make the most of it.

Hopefully, Mark would be impressed with what he saw when he came over. Jack wanted to show him what his foster son was good at. Mark was already proud of Stevie, and this would certainly have him smiling. Jack wanted to see that smile of Mark's light up his face. Preferably in his direction, but he would take what he could get.

Being around Mark every day this week and unable to say or do what he really wanted to do made Jack uncomfortable. He knew there were two kids around them all the time, and Jack knew he was not a quiet person. Talk about a mood killer. He adored Stevie and Christy, but they weren't exactly helping him right now.

Maybe he should suggest to Mark that he came over when the kids were at their foster grandmother's or had a babysitter. They would then be able to do something that involved a lot of noise. From the way Mark looked at him, Jack knew he would be more than up for it.

Having a handsome guy so close, but unable to touch him as he wanted, was more tense than he expected.

Jack was heading towards his office when he heard Stevie calling him. He didn't sound happy. Changing direction, Jack stepped out onto the back patio. Stevie was standing in the middle of the lawn being faced down by Denise Banfield. Stevie was starting to hit a growth spurt, but he was nothing compared to Denise's tall stature. And she was towering over him, waving a finger in his face as she said something in a hushed snarl.

How the hell had she managed to get in? The only other way into the back yard was around the side, and the gate was always locked. She had to have vaulted it to get inside. And now she was berating a child?

Jack bit back a growl.

"Mrs. Banfield!"

Denise spun around, almost falling over. She was wearing suede boots with thick heels along with black leggings and a light gray sweater dress. She did look good, but the anger in her eyes had Jack pulling up. She did not look right, and that had Jack wishing he had his gun.

"Mr. McGuire!" Denise huffed and stalked over to him. "I was beginning to think you weren't here."

"How did you get in here? The gate was locked."

"It was unlocked, actually."

Jack didn't believe that for a minute. He glanced over his shoulder at Stevie, who was shaking. If he were thirteen and confronted by a very tall and angry woman, he would be scared as well.

"Stevie, would you go inside? I'll just be a moment."

Stevie nodded and scurried indoors, giving Denise a wide berth. Denise watched him go with a sneer.

"Do you normally have kids do your work?" she scoffed.

"Stevie's the kid of a friend. He needs something to do."

"Why isn't he in school?"

Jack folded his arms and gave the woman a sharp glare. She had invaded his home and berated a child. That was not okay.

"What are you doing here, Mrs. Banfield?"

"I went to your office and that redheaded bitch said you're not there."

"I'm out of the office until Monday, and you shouldn't be here. How did you get my address?"

"Your secretary gave it to me."

Jack highly doubted that.

"Josie is my fellow PO, not my secretary, and she wouldn't have told you my address."

Denise shrugged.

"I'm resourceful. I needed to talk to you."

"If this is about your son..."

"Why else would I be here?" Denise's defiance melted a little and she started to turn on the waterworks. Jack was startled at how quickly she changed. "He didn't mean anything by it, Mr. McGuire. If you want to blame anyone for this, blame me. I got things wrong, and I regret it. Lucas is a good boy."

"You call what he did acceptable, then?"

"They were lying. They just freaked out when their parents found out."

Jack couldn't believe what he was hearing. She was actually putting the blame on the children? People who blamed the kids in that situation always made him sick to the stomach.

"Mrs. Banfield, are you seriously going to lay the blame for your son's crimes on innocent children? Think very carefully before you answer because you won't like my response."

Denise blinked and she faltered. Good, at least she knew when to back down a little. Jack could see where Lucas and Tracey got their mentality from. Denise thought she could get whatever she wanted and not take responsibility for her actions. He wondered if anyone actually stood up to her and called her out.

Not without repercussions on their end, certainly.

Denise's faltering didn't last long. She planted her hands on her hips and pouted.

"Lucas didn't do anything. This was all working against him to screw up his life."

"Oh, so people are now out to get him for some perceived slight, are they?"

"It has to be. Lucas has never committed a crime in his life. He didn't know what prison was before he was thrown in that hellhole."

Jack didn't bite on that. He had seen Lucas' record as a juvenile and it wasn't good. He was a sex offender in the making, certainly. Jack wouldn't be surprised if Denise had been egging him on the whole time. Just thinking about it made him feel sick.

He took a deep breath and let it out slowly. It was either that or put his hands around the woman's neck.

"Your son committed a crime. He's not the angel you claimed him to be. He went to jail, which is where he needed to be. If he wanted to be free for good, there was a set list of conditions he had to follow. If Lucas can't do that, he's not going to get freedom. Lucas needs to understand that. As do you, seeing as you think he should get away with it all because he loves you."

Denise's nostrils flared. She clearly didn't like being called out. She and Lucas really were related. Jack wondered for how many years had Denise been fighting Lucas' battles when he could do it himself. It was no wonder he was still doing as his mommy said.

Then she changed. Denise took a deep breath and fixed a smile. Stepping towards Jack, she rested a hand on his chest.

"Isn't there anything you can do to help him?" She gave him a coquettish look. "I'm sure there is something we could do to sort this out."

She was actually...Jack stepped back abruptly, backing up until he hit the back door. Dear God, she had come here to try and get him to think with the wrong head. She was that brazen about it.

How the fuck did she think that was okay?

"Get out of here now. Before I arrest you. And if you break anything on the way out, you'll be arrested for vandalism."

It took a moment for Denise to realize that she had been rejected. She looked rather bewildered, her mouth opening and closing like a fish. Then her eyes narrowed and she bared her teeth.

"Bastard."

"Out."

Jack had no idea how she got in, but he wasn't about to let her through the house. Denise huffed, and stomped her foot. Then she turned and headed around the side of the house. Jack heard the gate open and close with a loud bang. He was sure he heard the sound of breaking wood, which had him groaning. The landlord wasn't going to be impressed with that.

"Jack?"

Jack turned. Stevie was in the doorway, giving him a quizzical look.

"How long have you been there?"

"Long enough." Stevie peered up at him. "Is that the mother of the guy you sent back to jail?"

"Yes."

"Are all the family crazy?"

Jack grunted.

"Pretty much."

Chapter Four

Mark put his laptop into its bag and zipped it up. Then he got to his feet, rolling his shoulders in relief. He had been hunched over for too long. A long, hot bath sounded like a good thing right now.

"Right, I'm off." Slinging his laptop strap over his shoulder, Mark waved at his coworkers in cubicles across the aisle from him. "Goodnight."

"Night, Mark."

Mark gave the two men and one woman a sympathetic look as he walked away. Not too long ago, that was him staying for overtime, nothing to go home to. Now he had kids, and he was looking forward to seeing them. They did make him feel better walking through the door, especially when Christy was still at the age where she ran to the door to hug him.

People had called him mad for taking on two children he didn't know, but they supported his decision. Mark felt it was his duty to make sure these kids got a better upbringing than what they had been given, and he liked to think he was doing a good job. And it felt good looking at Stevie and Christy and seeing what he had done.

All children deserve a good childhood, and Mark would do that for all the kids he came across. But there was only so much he could do. Sometimes, there were instances where he couldn't do anything at all, and he had to watch helplessly as the children went back to an abusive situation even though he argued that it wasn't a good idea. Those phone calls telling him that a child had been killed not long after going back were the ones that came close to breaking him.

It made Mark more determined to make sure he kept children in a safer environment. Which made people like Tracey Banfield calling to falsely accuse someone slide down the ladder, in his opinion. To accuse another parent of neglect or abuse to get back at them was petty and dangerous. Mark hated those calls, but he had to investigate it all. Joe Swarbrick understood, although he had been fed up with it. Just one look at his house and his kids and Mark knew he was on a false call. One look at Tracey and that said everything.

She might have been a good person at one point. Hell, she might have been fantastic. But Mark didn't see that when he looked at her. He saw a woman who was caught up in drugs, and she was sliding further into a spiral that would make things worse than they already are.

He wouldn't be surprised if Lucas Banfield had been the one to supply Tracey the drugs. When he went to jail and Tracey moved away, she had cleaned up and turned into a stable person. But as soon as she came back, she slipped back. A slip-up on Joe's part, but Joe hadn't realized the extent of Tracey's addiction. He didn't even know it was there, so to have her acting out and cheating on him was out of character.

If she started doing it after years of bliss, then there was a good chance it had been happening before they met. It wasn't easy for a leopard to change their spots, not without a lot of pain. And Tracey didn't seem the type of person who would change so readily, if her outbursts in court were anything to go by.

Mark was glad his family had been normal. Nothing that made his life feel like a soap opera or massive drama. It was warm, loving and Mark was glad to have had it. He didn't think he would be strong enough to go through the things some of the kids he kept an eye on suffered with.

He needed to stop thinking about work. He was about to go home and see his family. Leave work in the office. Mark had promised that when he brought Stevie and Christy into the house for the first time; work would be left at the office. For the most part, he did that. They deserved his full attention. And they didn't deserve to hear about the fuckups Mark had to deal with on a daily basis.

Fishing out his keys, Mark headed into the parking garage. Soon, he would be home and they would be ordering takeout. Perhaps Jack would be joining them; he had done so for the rest of the week. Mark smiled. He liked having Jack around. Once the kids were in their rooms, the two of them would be up talking for hours. Mark was reluctant to see Jack go, but he had to get him to leave; if he didn't, the two of them would end up in bed, and Mark wasn't the quiet type.

God, to get that huge hunk of a man into bed...

Mark pushed that aside. Not that right now. He was not going to drive home with a hard-on. Focus on something else. Something mundane.

Easier said than done.

Mark's car was parked in the middle of the level, right under a light. Mark was halfway there when he heard a loud bang from across the garage. He jumped, spinning round at the sound. Mark scanned the garage, but saw nothing. The place was still full of cars, but there was nobody around.

"Is someone there?" Mark squinted into the darkness on the next level. That light was always flickering out. "If this is you, Jarvis, it's not funny."

That bastard from the office above liked to prank everyone else. He was a pain in the backside. Mark wondered how he got any work done at all when all he did was prank the guys and flirt with the women. Jack had told of a time when Jarvis attempted to flirt with Josie and actually put his hand on her backside while talking to her. Josie had promptly punched him in the groin, and Jarvis had been sent back to his own building walking like a constipated penguin.

Some people just didn't learn.

There was no noise after that. Mark waited and listened, but there was nothing. It was probably another one of the bulbs blowing. That had been happening, and they hadn't been replaced. It was getting harder to find a well-lit level to park his car on.

Mark turned to walk back to his car. Only to have something explode in the back of his head. Pain shot through his skull and the whole world tilted so fast Mark couldn't right himself. He crashed into the ground, squashing his hand underneath him. Pain shot up his arm, and again in his head when it bounced off the concrete. Another explosion of pain shot through his back as something hit him. Mark felt like the air had been sucked out of him. He lay there gasping, wanting to curl into a ball from the pain but wasn't sure what to protect first.

He was vaguely aware of someone shouting, and then there was the clattering of something metal and running footsteps. Mark tried to curl up, but his body hurt too much to move. He felt sick, his head felt like it had been split open, and he was struggling to breathe.

Footsteps came running at him, and someone was kneeling at his side. Small, warm hands touched his face, and Mark was aware of a female voice close by.

"Mark? Mark, look at me."

Mark managed to turn his head, and his vision cleared for a moment to see Josie leaning over him. Thank God for that. He tried to speak, but no sound came out. Then the pain in his head got too much and he closed his eyes.

***

Jack was furious. Someone had attacked Mark in the parking garage and he had passed out. Now he wanted to come home instead of going to the hospital. Jack couldn't believe what he was hearing when Josie called him. Mark needed to be seen by a doctor, he shouldn't be coming home and scaring the kids. It was like the knock to his head had made things worse and made him lose his common sense.

Stevie and Christy didn't deserve to see this. Mark had to know that.

But Mark was still insistent on going home, so Josie had agreed to drive him back. And then Jack would stay to keep an eye on him. No arguments on that. Mark might protest, but Jack wasn't budging. If the idiot was going to risk his health, he needed someone to watch over him. And Jack wasn't going to leave that to anyone else.

There was a knock at the door shortly after Josie texted him to say they were here, and Jack got up from the couch to answer it. But Christy got there first, and before Jack could tell her to leave it, she had opened the door. Then she stood there staring at Mark leaning on Josie, blood on his face.

"Oh, my God. Mark!"

"I'm fine, Christy." Mark eased off Josie and made his way into the house. He was swaying a little. "It's okay."

Jack couldn't believe what he was hearing. Mark looked like he had been in a fight. Christy looked like she was about to cry. Squeezing her shoulder, Jack directed Christy back towards the living room.

"You go and stay with your brother, Christy. I'll take care of this."

A tear trickling down her cheek, Christy went. Then Jack saw Stevie in the living room doorway, staring at Mark with such a white face it was a wonder he was still upright. The poor boy looked frightened. Jack turned to Josie.

"I'll take him now, Josie. Thanks for getting him back."

"He should be going to a hospital." Josie scowled at Mark as she stepped back. "He got whacked with a metal pipe. He could have brain damage."

"I'm okay. I've just got a headache." Mark stumbled towards the kitchen, pushing past Jack. "I just need to clean myself up."

"Like I said," Josie went on, "he could have brain damage. And I think that's a distinct possibility."

Jack sighed.

"You know what Mark's like. I'll take care of him."

"I'm sure you will." Josie smirked.

"Josie."

"Fine, I'm going." Josie glanced towards the living room door. "I'm sorry about the kids having to see this. I didn't want to scare them, but Mark wouldn't let me clean him up."

"You let me worry about him, okay?" Jack kissed Josie's head. "Thanks for your help."

Josie grunted and headed towards the door, shutting the door a little too hard. She was pissed, and you didn't need to be a psychic to know that. Jack sighed and headed into the kitchen. Mark had got out a first-aid kit from the cupboard and was sitting at the center counter opening up the antiseptic wipes. Jack shook his head and plucked the packet from Mark's fingers.

"You needed to go to a hospital, Mark."

"I don't need a hospital. I just need to clean up and I'll be fine." Mark scowled. "Stop delaying this, Jack. I want to just wipe this blood off. It's not that bad."

"Not that bad? You scared the kids! You think they wanted to see that?"

Mark faltered. His head had to be jumbled if he hadn't thought about that. Jack ripped the packet open and followed where the blood was coming from. The cut was in the back of his head. Mark had to have been unconscious for a while to have it dripping down his face.

"I passed out in the car again." Mark wiped at his face with his sleeve. "I didn't have blood on my face when I got into Josie's car."

"I'm sure Josie will send you the bill for bleeding all over her Boxster."

Mark grunted. Then he sat up, almost catching Jack in the face with his head.

"My laptop! Where is it? I dropped it when I got hit."

"Don't panic, Josie put it inside the door as she left. I'm sure it bounced sufficiently." Jack gently shoved Mark forward, making him lean over the counter. "Now stay still. I don't want a headache myself."

Mark grumbled, but he stayed quiet as Jack cleaned the wound. It wasn't too bad a cut, but it had been bleeding quite heavily. Mark was going to feel woozy for a while.

"Does anything else hurt?"

"My back." Mark winced as Jack tugged some matted hair away from the wound. "They walloped me one with something that must've been a pipe."

"You could have some internal injuries, Mark."

"Just a lot of bruising."

"More than a lot of bruising." Jack leaned closer to inspect the wound. "Someone whacked you pretty good. I'm surprised your skull didn't cave in."

"It took me by surprise." Mark grumbled. He was slumped on the counter. "Didn't even see it coming."

Jack could feel a chill down his back. Another surprise attack in a parking garage. Mark always took precautions, and kept himself safe. Why was this any different? He picked up a big square bandage and pressed it to the back of Mark's head, using tape to keep it in place.

"After what happened to Judge Harvey at the courthouse, do you think it was a good idea to go out into a parking garage alone?"

"Jack, it wasn't the same garage and it wasn't the same person."

"You still got attacked." Jack jerked back as Mark flinched again. "For God's sake, stop being such a baby."

"Sorry, but I'm not good when people prod at the injured bits."

Jack didn't respond to that. He stepped around and began to gather the supplies, putting it back into the first-aid kit. Mark straightened up, grimacing as he started to shrug out of his jacket. Jack gave him a sidelong glance.

"Do you need any help?"

"No, I'm fine." Mark stopped for a moment, took a deep breath, and then slid the jacket down his arms. "It's probably a disgruntled parent pissed off at CPS and I was an unlucky target."

"Disgruntled parents go after you?"

"Wouldn't be the first time."

Now Jack felt even colder. Mark had never mentioned this to him before. He took a breath and let it out slowly. It was either that or lose his temper at Mark for treating this so lightly.

"Are you calling the cops?"

"I've called Rusty. He's going to come here to take my statement." Mark slid off the stool and moved gingerly into the hall. "I've got it under control, and Rusty is reliable."

Jack knew about that. But Mark's brother was a homicide cop and Mark was very much alive. Aside from taking a statement, he couldn't do much except pass it to those who dealt with these types of crimes. Mark hung up his jacket behind the door of his office and slumped into his chair with a heavy sigh. Jack stood in the door and watched him. Mark looked exhausted. It was a wonder he hadn't keeled over yet.

"You should've told me that people come after you."

Mark snorted.

"For you to do what? Stand there and stare at them? That's all you need to do sometimes."

"I can be scary when I need to be." Jack said sharply. "And you need to be more careful."

"So I should hide behind you if I get hurt again?" Mark sneered.

Jack bristled.

"That's not what I meant. But it's best that you don't go out alone. You don't carry a gun or any type of self-defense weapon."

"I have a baseball bat in the car."

"How's that supposed to help when you're not anywhere near the car? You can't exactly carry that around, can you?"

Mark glared at him. Then he turned away and glowered at the blank computer screen. Goddammit, Jack wanted to shake him. His ego was bruised from the attack, but Jack would rather have his ego bruised than have his skull completely split open.

Leaving the office room, Jack went over to the living room and went in. Stevie and Christy were

70

sitting on the couch, the game they had been playing up on the screen. But nobody was playing, the controllers on the coffee table. Stevie was sat hunched over, elbows on his knees as he glared at the floor. Christy was curled up beside her brother, arms wrapped around her middle as she sank against the cushions. She looked up as Jack came in and sat up.

"Is Mark okay?"

"He'll be fine. I think he's more wound up that he got jumped."

"It couldn't be Dad, could it?" Stevie asked, lifting his head. "He's not out and coming after us, is he?"

Jack blinked.

"No, it wouldn't be your dad. He's not given any possibility of parole."

"But he could have escaped." Stevie insisted.

"You would've been notified if that was the case. Chances are it's someone else Mark's inadvertently pissed off." Jack looked from Stevie to Christy. "If I call Amber, do you want to spend the weekend at her place if she says yes?"

"I would, but..." Christy bit her lip. Her eyes were shining with tears again. "I'm not sure if I want to leave Mark."

Jack's heart melted. She was far too young to be worrying about so much.

"He'll be fine, Christy. But he might have a concussion, and it's not fair on you two to keep an eye on him. Mark needs rest himself."

"We can take care of ourselves." Stevie said. "I'm thirteen, so I can do that."

71

Jack smiled.

"I remember the last time you were at home on your own. I don't think Mark would appreciate having to deal with that mess right now."

Stevie pouted.

"It was just a one-off."

"Until then, you let Mark decide when he can trust you to not blow something up."

Stevie didn't like that. Jack could understand. If he were thirteen and told he couldn't stay home alone, he wouldn't have been happy. But he had already been close to six feet at that age and was on the wrestling team. Stevie was half his size and skinny. The kid was going to shoot up eventually, but he did not look thirteen. Give him six months, and that would change, but he had made some daft decisions in just a few hours, and Mark wanted to wait until he was at least fourteen before he tried again.

Stevie clearly wanted something else, but he wasn't going to get it. Mark was the parent, and Jack was going to respect that.

"Just humor me, Stevie, will you? Your foster dad's not going to be much fun, anyway."

"Hey!"

Jack turned. Mark was in the doorway to his office glaring at him. Sighing, Jack looked at Christy.

"Call Amber, will you, Christy?" As Christy got off the couch and went to the cordless phone in the corner, Jack turned back to Mark. "You know I'm right, Mark. You can't look after the kids when you're injured. What if I need to take you to the hospital?"

"They're ten and thirteen. They can take care of themselves."

"Thank you!" Stevie declared. "At least, someone remembers!"

"Stevie." Jack focused on Mark. "This is serious, Mark. You could've had your skull split open, and it's not fair on children to see you end up in a coma because you're not taking care of yourself. You need to focus on you, not put it on your kids."

Mark looked like he wanted to argue, his scowl still there. Then he looked away. Jack waited. They could argue about this all night, but Jack wasn't about to leave Mark here on his own with the children. And if someone had attacked Mark and came back again, Jack didn't want Stevie and Christy anywhere near it. Mark had to know if repercussions happened, the children would be caught in the middle.

Finally, Mark's shoulders slumped and he looked away with a scowl.

"Just make sure Stevie and Christy are safe first, okay?"

Jack relaxed a little. He could do that.

Chapter Five

Stevie and Christy still weren't happy, but they packed a few things and were ready by the time Amber arrived. Christy clung onto Mark like she didn't want to let go, her face buried into his shirt. Stevie just stood by looking sullen. Mark felt awful for both of them, but Jack was right. If whoever attacked him in the parking garage came after him and knew where he lived, they would be caught in the crossfire. And with Mark the way he was, he wouldn't be able to protect them.

He hated feeling weak and useless. They deserved better.

Amber got there pretty quickly and the kids got into the car. Christy huddled up against her brother. Mark tried not to look. The two of them had never seen him like this before, and their homelife had been relatively calm aside from a few fights on Stevie's side. This had to shake them up. He didn't want to think what was going through their heads right now.

His mother squeezed Mark's arm.

"They'll be okay with me. I can take them to school on Monday, if you want."

"I'm sure I'll be fine by Sunday, Mom." Mark hugged the older woman. "It's just for tonight, unless Jack starts being regimental about it."

"All right." Amber drew back and glanced towards the car. "Christy's scared. They both are."

"I know. I'll call them later."

Amber nodded. She had sounded horrified when Mark told her what happened. It had been a few years since Mark had been attacked, but it hadn't been as bad as this. Amber still worried over her eldest son, even though Mark could easily look after himself. But now he was beginning to realize that it didn't matter how old the child was, the mother would always worry.

"You've done a good job with them, Mark."

"Why are you saying that, Mom?"

"Because I can see the cogs whirling. You're worried you're doing something wrong."

Mark sighed.

"I hate that you know what I'm thinking sometimes, Mom."

"I know." Amber cupped his jaw. "They'll be okay, just as long as they know you're going to be there for them. They've been through a lot and you're a steady influence."

"I know. And I will be."

There was no way in hell that he was going anywhere. Mark stepped back as Amber got behind the wheel and backed her car down his driveway. He was glad to have a mother close by who would drop everything for him, within reason. It wasn't just him that was a steady influence in Stevie and Christy's lives.

And Amber wasn't likely to get walloped over the head.

Mark watched the car disappear around the corner before going inside. He double locked the door and put the outside alarm on. Even then, he didn't feel entirely safe, but the knowledge his foster kids were out of a potentially bad situation did make him feel a little better.

Which was more than could be said for his head. That still hurt like hell.

Pushing off the door, Mark went into the living room. Jack was drawing the curtains, switching on the standing lamp in the corner. He looked like he had been working hard all day, his t-shirt and jeans sweaty and covered in dust. Mark hadn't noticed that when he first came in.

"What have you been doing all day?"

"Sorting out the back yard with Stevie. Ended up being a bit more work than I expected." Jack crossed the room. "Did they go okay?"

"Just about." Mark went to rub the back of his head to ease the itching, but then remembered he couldn't. "Christy's crying, and Stevie is angry."

"That's understandable. They've had stability for the last two years with you and that's gotten shaken for them. They're just nervous."

"We're cool. I'm not going anywhere."

Jack's expression softened.

"I know that." He squeezed Mark's shoulder. "I saw you do a lot of good stuff, Mark. They're good kids, and a credit to you."

"I'm glad." That did make Mark feel a little better. "I'm glad I took the chance to foster them."

And it felt good having Jack touch him like this. Mark could feel the need building to have Jack touching him everywhere, not just his shoulder. But he had just been attacked and his head was pounding. How could he think about sex or anything intimate right now? Mark moved away and slumped onto the couch, leaning his head gingerly onto the cushions. It hurt for a moment but then it became a gentle, comfortable throbbing. God, his head was going to be more than a bit sore in the morning.

"Can I ask you something, Mark?"

"Depends what you want to ask." Mark arched an eyebrow at Jack. "Is it a dirty question?"

Jack blinked.

"Should you even be thinking about dirty stuff right now?"

"My mind's all scrambled. I think you could ask me anything and I would answer it without any filter."

"I'll remember that." Jack folded his arms. "Why did you take those two on? What was so special about them?"

Mark frowned.

"I'm still not sure, even now. Their case...it kind of hit me in the gut. There was a connection there, and I didn't want to see them separated. They needed to be together. All they had after their parents were arrested and their grandparents refused to take them in was each other. I didn't want to see them split up."

"You think they would have been split up?"

Mark nodded. He had seen it far too many times.

"Believe it or not, while there are a lot of foster parents, there are quite a few who are very picky with what they want in terms of children. They want babies or they want only little girls or teenagers, they won't take siblings if they are different genders..."

"Are you kidding me on that one?"

"Sadly, no. Christy might have gotten a home, but Stevie wouldn't. That's not fair to him. I wanted them to be together, and when no one would take them both, not even their grandparents, I said I would."

Mark wasn't registered as a foster parent when he said he wanted to take them in, but he got the paperwork pushed through and pulled a few strings. Less than a week later, Stevie and Christy were leaving the group home they had been temporarily put in and were in his house. That first week had been difficult with everyone sizing each other up, but three years on and Mark didn't regret it. He would do it all again.

He just hoped he didn't lose them after all this. There was a chance he could, and Mark didn't want to go there.

Jack was silent for a moment. Then he went over to the mantelpiece. Mark had stuck up their most recent school pictures, which had Stevie actually smiling in a photograph when he was normally scowling. Jack stared at them.

"I don't know why Stevie wouldn't get taken in. He's a great kid. I like him."

"He likes you, too." Mark grunted. "More than me, I think."

"You're their foster parent, Mark." Jack turned. "He's always going to like you first."

Mark hoped that were true. And it was going to take a long time to get Stevie to completely trust him. They had come a long way since that first day, and Mark wanted to keep that. Stevie may not openly admit it, but he wanted a solid male figure in his life to look up to. Mark wanted that to be him.

They stared at each other, and Mark was beginning to get very aware that it was just them now. They were alone. If he were feeling fit enough, Mark would have jumped Jack right now. But he didn't think his head would be able to cope with it. He needed some painkillers.

Then his stomach growled. He needed food as well. Jack grinned.

"Hungry?"

"Starving." Mark sighed. "I guess I'm going to have to figure out what to eat. It's normally takeout evening, but it's not as fun without the kids."

"Sorry, you'll have to make do with me." Jack got out his cell phone. "Burgers, curry or Thai?"

"Burgers. I fancy gorging on some meat." God, did that actually sound more sexual than it should have been? Mark cleared his throat. "In the meantime, what are we going to do while I figure out if I have a concussion?"

"Well, we can play a few games."

Mark groaned.

"Not video games. I don't think I can handle the bright lights or the noise right now."

"I had something else in mind." Grinning, Jack left the room. "Give me a moment."

"What are...?"

But Jack was already gone, leaving Mark confused. What was he up to? Jack returned a few minutes later with a long, flat box that looked a bit worse for wear. It took a moment for Mark to realize what it was.

"Monopoly?"

"Christy found it in the games cupboard earlier. She asked about it."

Mark groaned.

"God, I forgot I had this game."

"I can tell." Jack blew the dust off the lid, sending a cloud into the air. He coughed. "It was on the top shelf of the cupboard and it hasn't been played in years, judging by how much dust there is on this."

"That's because I hate monopoly."

"Why do you keep it, then?"

Mark's nose tickled from the dust, and he sneezed.

"I kept it so Stevie and Christy can have an adult game to play. They're at the age where they can play it now, but I forgot about it."

"Because you hate it."

"Damn right I do."

A slow grin passed across Jack's face. Now Mark was on the alert. So was his cock, which was waking up to that devastating smile. What was he up to?

"You haven't played monopoly the way I do. Adults only, of course, but it's a lot more fun than the regular way."

"Huh! How can you make monopoly more interesting?"

Jack put the box onto the coffee table and began to gather the stuff on the table, moving it to the armchair. He was still grinning.

"Instead of using money for rent, you use your clothes."

It took a moment for Mark to realize what he had just said. He stared.

"Did...are you suggesting that we play strip monopoly?"

"Yep." Jack went onto his knees on the other side of the table and took the lid off the box. "I got the idea when I watched *Friday the 13th* when I was a kid."

"You got the idea for a strip game from a horror movie?"

"Essentially." Jack brought out the board and unfolded it. "The movie didn't get to the good bits, so I thought I'd give it a try. Made things very interesting when I was at university."

"How interesting?"

"I got laid each time." Jack waggled his eyebrows. "People can't seem to resist me. I don't know what I do, but I seem to be a magnet."

Maybe because you're hot and big all over. Mark swallowed and looked away. Then he realized what Jack had said. He got laid each time he played a strip game? Was that his way of saying he was playing a seduction game?

Mark felt the warmth of the room tickling his skin. Jack wanted to play? Mark could do that. He grinned.

"Okay. I'll get the takeout in and you set up. If you're not afraid of stripping off in front of me."

"I'm not afraid." Jack's eyes darkened as he looked over Mark, his gaze raking over Mark's body before pausing on Mark's hardened crotch. "Are you?"

81

For a moment, Mark struggled to breathe. He knew Jack could be intense, but never like this. He swallowed.

"I like a challenge."

***

"This is going better than I expected."

Mark groaned as he undid his pants and started to slide them down his legs.

"That's because you've got most of the squares."

"Good tactic, isn't it?"

Jack's eyes were sparkling. Mark rolled his eyes and tossed his pants into Jack's face. The bastard knew exactly what he was doing. When they first started, Jack began to pick as many areas as he could to put his hotels on. He used all his money to pay for the hotels and Mark realized too late that pretty much every other square he landed on would result in Mark losing an item of clothing.

They had only been playing for fifteen minutes and Jack had only lost his shirt and both his shoes, though Mark was naked except for his boxers. Mark tried to concentrate, but he kept getting distracted by Jack's naked chest. Man, it was magnificent. Jack wanted to rub his hands over that hairless chest, lick him all over. No wonder the guy got laid each time he played a strip game; no one would be able to resist a big naked guy like Jack McGuire sitting so close.

At least they had eaten before getting on with the game; Mark didn't think he would be able to manage to eat anything if he saw Jack get naked beforehand. He would be drooling too much.

Mark had given up hiding his erection now. It would be practically impossible the less clothes he had on, and now his cock was standing to attention, tenting his boxers. Jack's eyes were now locked onto Mark's crotch, his expression darkening to a hunger Mark had never seen before. Damn, this was hotter than he anticipated. And his head wasn't hurting anymore, not with the painkillers and the anticipation that he was finally getting Jack naked.

Or rather, Jack was getting him naked.

"Maybe we should've said one button at a time." Mark resisted the urge to rub a hand over his cock. "That would make things a bit fairer."

"You giving up now?"

"Does it look like I'm giving up?"

Jack's grin widened.

"Looks like you're enjoying the game more than you expected."

"I'm not going to be able to look at this game again."

Jack chuckled.

"I still don't. I just can't play it regularly now." He swiped the two dice. "My turn."

He rolled, and moved his little metal shoe around the board. It landed on one of Mark's few hotels, which had Mark grinning. At least he was losing some clothes. Jack rose to his feet and undid his jeans. Mark's mouth went dry and he couldn't look away as Jack pushed his jeans down his thighs, finally kicking them aside. He was sure his eyes were popping out of his head as he looked over every sleek solid muscle of Jack's body.

"You're not wearing underwear."

"I was until I went to the bathroom while you were getting the takeout." Jack curled a hand around his huge cock and stroked himself. "I wanted to have a few less clothes to take off."

Mark's eyes were glued to Jack's cock as the other man pumped himself. Holy hell, he was huge. He had to be almost as thick as Mark's wrist, and Mark wasn't skinny by any means. When Mark had wondered if Jack was big all over, he never expected that big.

It's going to be incredible when I take that cock.

"I think someone's still a little overdressed." Jack stepped around the desk and knelt between Mark's spread thighs. His fingers slid over Mark's boxers to the waistband. "Want some help?"

"I haven't rolled yet."

But Mark didn't stop him and lifted his hips when Jack gave the boxers a bit of a tug. Jack peeled the boxers down Mark's legs, tossing them aside. He gasped as Jack put a huge hand around Mark's cock and stroked him.

"Let's call it paying rent in advance."

He rose up on his knees and kissed him. Mark found himself leaning into the kiss, which made every part of his body shiver. Jack's mouth was soft but very hot, and his kiss was so sensual Mark could feel his own resolve breaking. He wanted more than slow and sweet. He wanted hot, hard and a lot of it. But Jack was in charge right now, so Mark clenched his hands on the cushions to stop himself from grabbing him.

Then Jack broke the kiss, kissing over Mark's jaw and neck before making his slow way down Mark's body. His tongue snaked out and flicked over Mark's nipples, sending more shockwaves through Mark's cock. When he finally got to Mark's cock, Mark was wound so tight he was sure he was going to cum as soon as Jack took him in. Jack shot him a sly grin as he licked the tip of Mark's cock.

"I think we can consider future rent paid off after this." He whispered.

Then he lowered his head, swallowing Mark's cock in one go. Mark was not a small guy, by any means, and previous partners had struggled to take him in completely. His cock hit the back of Jack's throat, but there was no floundering. He barely stopped as he rose his head up and then back down. Mark's head was spinning and it wasn't from his supposed concussion. His heart was going to come out of his chest if Jack kept doing this.

His hands went to Jack's bald head and pressed down as he lifted his hips. Jack moaned, but he didn't fight it. The sensation of him going further down Jack's throat and his mouth tightening had Mark's lust curling up even tighter than before. Fuck, that felt incredible.

"Jack…" Mark's head fell back, not caring that he was bothering his head injury. "Jack, more."

Jack made a noise that could have been growling, and he began to suck harder. He met Mark's thrusts without even faltering, the tightening around Mark's cock making Mark's chest tighten. Fuck, he was going to explode in a moment.

Then Jack's fingers brushed over Mark's balls and he pressed a finger into Mark's ass, thrusting at the same time as Mark's thrusts. That sent Mark's pleasure over the edge and he came with a shout, feeling his release hit the back of Jack's throat. He wanted to come down from something so intense, but Jack kept wringing it out, fucking his ass with his finger while his mouth drank in everything he took.

Mark didn't think he could take anymore, but he wanted to. Fuck, he wanted a lot more of it. Once he got his breath back.

With one final lick, Jack eased off Mark's cock and his hand disappeared from Mark's ass. He crawled up Mark's body and took his mouth in a firm kiss. Someone was shaking, and Mark couldn't figure out if it was him or Jack. Jack broke the kiss with a grin.

"What do you think now?"

Mark was surprised either of them could talk. He cupped Jack's head, running his hands over Jack's smooth scalp.

"I think I've found something more interesting to do instead of monopoly."

Chapter Six

The need to use the bathroom woke Mark the next morning. He crawled out of bed and headed to the bathroom. It was a wonder he could use his legs after the night before. Jack certainly knew how to make a man come over and over until he was close to passing out. Mark didn't think that was possible, and he wasn't about to argue. Even now, his skin was tingling with the after-effects of the orgasms. And they had fallen asleep at two that morning.

How did they wait two years for this? They should have done this long ago.

After washing up in the bathroom, Mark headed back to the bedroom. Jack was still asleep, sleeping on his belly with his arms propping up the pillow. The duvet was kicked aside, the corner barely covering his backside. Mark had worshipped that body, and his own body was stirring again at the sight. Jack was a beautiful sight to see.

And Mark got to see it a lot.

His cock was hard again. Picking up the bottle of lube from the floor by the bed and an unopened condom packet, Mark opened the packet and rolled the condom over his cock, squirting a generous amount of lube onto his hand. Stroking his cock, Mark climbed onto the bed and started kissing his way up Jack's back. Jack sighed, but he didn't seem to stir much. Mark kissed and nipped at the back of Jack's neck with his teeth as he inserted his finger into Jack's ass. Jack sighed and lifted his hips.

"That's nice."

"You haven't had nice yet." Mark added another finger and picked up the thrusts. "I can't get enough of this ass."

"I can tell." Jack groaned, his ass muscles tightening around Mark's fingers. "I hope you're planning on doing more, or I'm going to be taking over."

"I love it when you take over." Mark withdrew his fingers and fisted his cock, pressing it to the tight entrance. "But it's my bed. You follow my rules."

Jack chuckled, breaking off with a gasp as Mark's cock slid in easily. Jack clutched onto the pillow, his back bowing as he pressed back.

"You...you weren't too bothered about that last night."

"Well, rules are changing." Mark rolled his hips, which had Jack groaning. "When we're at your apartment, you can dictate what we do."

"Just shut up and fuck me."

Jack was practically shaking. Mark kept it slow, rolling his hips as he pumped into Jack's ass, keeping his thrusts slow but deep. Jack growled, bucking underneath Mark as he tried to push back, but he didn't pick up the pace. He kissed and licked his way along Jack's back, smiling as Jack's moans got louder and more insistent.

"I thought I said fuck me, not screw me slowly."

Mark chuckled and cupped Jack's hip, pressing him into the bed.

"Like I said, I'm in charge. And I'm going to make you come like this."

With his head pounding as it was, Mark didn't think he could go too fast, anyway. He closed his eyes and enjoyed the feel of Jack's ass tightening hard around his cock. That had happened during the night and the feel was not getting boring.

Holy fuck, Jack was going to wring him out completely at this rate.

"Mark…" Jack was panting hard. "I'm going to cum again."

So was Mark. Moments after Jack spoke, his orgasm exploded, warmth ricocheting up his back and through his cock. He thrust one more time as his cock twitched. Jack's body was trembling. Mark could tell he was close. Pulling out quickly, Mark flipped Jack onto his back and took Jack's cock into his mouth. Jack let out a shout, and his release filled Mark's mouth, his hands grabbing Mark's head and trying to press him down. Mark took in all of him, licking up every drop, finishing with a last long lick up Jack's cock before kissing his way up Jack's chest. He could feel a heart racing under his lips.

Jack was smiling as Mark reached his mouth, taking Mark's kiss still with a smile.

"You know how to wake someone up, don't you?"

Mark grinned.

"I aim to please." He shifted to Jack's side and took off the condom, leaning over to drop it into the trash can by his bed. "You don't mind, do you?"

"Of course not." Jack was watching Mark as he turned back. "You know I've thought about this since we met?"

Mark stared.

"You serious?"

"Yeah." Jack gave him a sheepish smile and shrugged. "Didn't think you'd want to be around a guy who deals with dangerous convicts all the time. I bring a lot of baggage."

That had Mark bursting into laughter.

"Have you seen the baggage I deal with? I also deal with criminals, just in a different way."

That had been his concern? Jack had to be daft to think that was even a problem. From the look on his face, Jack was beginning to realize that. He had been making a worry over nothing.

"I should've said something before, shouldn't I?"

"Yes, you should have." Mark leaned over and kissed him. "Think you can handle two kids with one going through the teenage hormones?"

Jack laughed. He slid his hand down Mark's chest and cupped his semi-erect cock.

"If I can handle you, I can handle them."

Mark groaned and he thrust into Jack's hand.

Jack had an uncanny ability to make some aroused so quickly after the last round. And Mark was getting there already. He straddled Jack's waist and kissed him, feeling Jack's hands flex and squeeze around his backside.

"You'd better get the lube." Mark reached back and stroked Jack's cock, which was starting to come back to life. "I think we're up for showing how much we can handle each other."

Jack laughed. Then he groaned when a ringing noise sounded through the house. It made Mark sit up abruptly at the sudden noise.

90

"What the fuck is that?"

"That's my cell phone." Jack lifted his hips and tipped Mark onto the bed. "I'd better get that."

"Why? It's the weekend."

"That's the ringtone for Josie. If she's calling on a Saturday, it's important." Jack flashed Mark a wink as he slid off the bed. "I won't be long."

"You'd better not be." Mark lay back and started stroking his cock. "I'll be ready when you get back."

Jack groaned. Then he hurried out of the room, his footsteps thundering down the stairs. Mark could hear him answer the phone in the living room, his deep voice floating up the stairs. Mark closed his eyes and listened, feeling himself stir even more at the sound of Jack's tone. He did have a lovely voice.

"You what? When did this happen?"

Mark stopped stroking and opened his eyes. That didn't sound good. Jack's voice had changed. He didn't sound so jovial anymore. Mark sat up. Something had happened, and it wasn't good.

Snatching up his boxers, Mark tugged them on and hurried downstairs. Jack was standing in the middle of the living room, the tension in his shoulders as he stood with his back to Mark.

"Okay, I'll be right there. Give me forty-five minutes."

Jack hung up. Mark moved in and touched his lover's back. Lover. Not a word he expected to use on Jack. It felt good, even in the current situation.

"What is it? Has something happened to Josie?"

"No, she's safe. She got a call from the guard to our building." Jack turned. "My office has been turned upside-down. I have to get down there now."

So much for having a day to themselves. But Mark wasn't about to let him go alone.

"I'm coming with you."

"Mark…"

"Don't argue. Besides," Mark threw over his shoulder as he headed up the stairs, "you need to keep an eye on me for concussion, remember?"

He could hear Jack mumbling something as he followed.

***

Jack had been looking forward to spending the day with Mark, preferably in bed. After taking the initiative and making a move, Jack was glad it had come to fruition. He had thought Mark would be dynamite in bed, but Jack had no idea how explosive it would be. And Mark's responsive nature made him feel good. Jack was surprised he was able to walk properly.

Now he was going to have to go in and sort out his office, which had been broken into. Their offices were always locked and security was always around, so how the fuck had someone managed to get in and make a mess without anyone noticing. That was what Jack was worried about right now. He and Josie had made their suite of offices tightly secure. To know someone had got into sensitive files and various documents was unnerving.

Mark sat beside him as Jack raced through the streets, trying not to go above the speed limit. His partner was silent, but Jack appreciated his presence.

It was stopping him from going completely mad and letting out his frustration by driving too fast, which was a problem Jack was struggling with. Having his lover there next to him had Jack feeling a little calmer.

Lover. Partner. Jack had wondered if he would ever call Mark those titles several times over the years. Now it was happening, and it felt good. It suited Mark.

Jack didn't broadcast his sexuality around, seeing it as nobody's business. A few select people knew, but everyone else had no idea. He wasn't concerned about people finding out that he was dating a guy, although he was sure a few of his parolees would end up getting upset about having a gay parole officer. They didn't get to choose a PO, so they would have to lump it. Jack could handle all that.

Just as long as he got to handle Mark when he wanted.

They pulled up in the parking garage that linked both of their buildings and Jack practically jogged into the elevator, Mark close behind him. Jack ended up hopping from foot to foot, hoping that it wasn't as bad as Josie said. Mark took his hand and gave it a squeeze.

"Calm down. Things are going to be okay."

"How do we know that? The cops have been called."

"We can sort it all out. At least nobody was there and got hurt."

That was something, but it didn't give Jack much comfort. He had a lot of sensitive information in those files. His parolees had things about them that he was meant to keep away from the public eye. He didn't need people finding out where they lived and going on a lynching. That had happened before, and Jack wasn't about to let it happen again.

He could only hope that whoever broke in didn't find what they were looking for.

They stepped out of the elevator and headed down the hall to Jack's offices. Mark let go as they reached the door, allowing Jack to go in first. Josie was pacing around the lobby, her face as red as her hair. She turned as Jack hurried to her.

"Where are the cops?"

"They're on their way right now." Josie brushed her hair away from her face. "They've said not to touch anything at all until after everything has been processed."

Which meant having their big boots stomping everywhere. Jack had had to deal with the cops before, and they often saw him as an extension of his parolees. Almost like he was a pimp for convicts. He didn't need them looking into his files.

"Can I at least go in?"

Josie gestured towards Jack's office door.

"Just don't touch anything. You might not be able to get in, either."

Then Jack saw why. The door was half open, jammed stuck by whatever was on the floor. He stuck his head around the door and his eyes widened when he saw the mess. His files were strewn all over the floor, papers scattered almost across every inch of the carpet. His computer chair was upended and the computer had been turned almost ninety degrees. The trophies Jack won for sharpshooting and wrestling had been knocked off the shelves, and there was a massive dent in the wall with the trophies lying in a pile on the floor. Someone had been throwing them. How had security not heard that?

Mark squeezed past and stuck his head in. He whistled.

"Wow. What train came through here?"

Jack drew back and turned to Josie.

"What the hell happened?"

"I have no idea." Josie bristled at his tone. "I came in to pick up my gear that I forgot, and I found this. I swear the place was locked, and Dwayne said he didn't hear anything."

"I'm sure." Jack muttered.

Josie flinched. She glared at him.

"We honestly didn't know! Don't take it out on me!"

"Take it easy, both of you." Mark got between them and turned to Jack. "Deep breaths, Jack. Don't lay blame with Josie. She had no idea."

"At least someone's on my side." Josie grunted.

Jack sighed and looked away. He was too worked up after finding his office turned inside-out. Josie may not have been at fault, but he needed someone to blame.

"Jack." Mark touched his face, causing Jack to look up at him. "How do we know what's been destroyed?"

"We don't until the cops have done their job and we can get in there."

Which would take forever, the damn cops liked to draw it out. Especially when Jack was involved. Common courtesy didn't seem to compute with them.

It looked like they were going to have to spend their weekend sorting everything out. Not exactly what he wanted after his confession to Mark.

Chapter Seven

The cops came and went, taking close to three hours. Jack found himself banished from his own offices while it was happening, so he and Mark had convened in Josie's office. He couldn't sit still, pacing back and forth to the point he was surprised he didn't wear out the carpet.

It wasn't the first time someone had gotten into his office and destroyed it, and it didn't make Jack feel any better. He hated his privacy violated. Other times, they discovered it was one of the convicts he was keeping an eye on, trying to find something that they could either use to their advantage or make disappear. Chances were it was the case this time, although Jack was having doubts. He had no idea why, but the doubts were there. Something else was going on, and Jack hated not knowing.

Thank God Mark was there. Josie had left at Mark's urging, and then he had stayed, mostly sitting in silence as Jack paced around and occasionally ranted. His presence was surprisingly comforting, even if he barely said a word. Jack was glad Mark was still there, that he had someone to keep watch. Some of the cops who had arrived had been sneering at Jack, and Jack didn't care for that. He did his job, and they were supposed to do theirs.

At least Mark's brother was a decent guy and good cop. Jack could cope with Rusty, just not his egotistical coworkers.

Finally, the cops left, taking their forensic team with them. Jack took a look inside his office once they left, and was surprised that the powder they used for fingerprints hadn't coated a thick layer over everything. It was certainly hanging in the air, the dust making Jack sneeze, but not as bad as he expected. He felt like he had dandruff after the last time. White powder on his bald head was not a good look.

So, he and Mark focused on getting the place tidied. Jack trusted Mark with the papers, and knew he could be discreet. Mark was not a person who would pass it around to all and sundry. Even convicts deserved their privacy, or what was left of it, and Jack liked to respect that as much as he could.

It was mid-afternoon by the time they finally got all the files in the right order. Jack slumped into his chair with a heavy sigh.

"God, I'm glad that's all finished." He looked at his watch. "And it only took just over six hours."

"Well, they're all put away and sorted." Mark closed the top drawer of the filing cabinet. "Have you noticed anything missing in particular?"

"You didn't see Lucas Banfield's files around, did you?"

"No. Where were they last?"

"In my top drawer in my desk." Jack gestured at his computer. "I checked all of the files with my digital files, and while Lucas' records are on my backup drive, they're not on the computer or in the paper files."

Mark frowned.

"They managed to delete computer files? I thought your computer was password protected."

"It was."

Jack couldn't understand how it was possible to get onto his computer. He had made sure there were passwords for practically everything, and the last time someone tried to get into his files, they couldn't get anything. Jack had been paranoid about that for years and had asked his sister, who was a computer whiz, to install something that would need only him to bypass if someone tripped anything. The idea was if it sensed that it wasn't Jack by typing in the wrong password or going into a sensitive file, the entire computer would shut down. But it had been on sleep when Jack had seen it. The cops swore they didn't touch it when Jack asked about it, but he didn't think they would have gone onto it. It was covered in powder for fingerprints, which would be an absolute nightmare to clean, but the only fingerprints on it were Jack's. Some of them were smudged, which said someone had used it, but there were no extra prints. Someone had to be wearing gloves.

His computer had been the target. Throwing everything else around just seemed to be a smokescreen. It wouldn't be the first time when someone tried to break into his office for information, either to obtain it to their advantage or delete it completely, but this was the first time it had looked this bad.

Mark knelt on the couch and looked over the back. Then he started to reach for something. For a moment, Jack was distracted by the flash of smooth skin just above the waistband of his jeans. Mark had simply thrown on a pair of old jeans with a bulky blue sweater. Nothing underneath it, so he had been flashing a lot of his stomach as he used the sweater to wipe his face of sweat. Had it been any other situation, Jack might have jumped him.

Get your head focused. Preferably the one on your shoulders.

"Found some more papers." Mark straightened up, a scattered sheaf of papers on his hand. "These look like miscellaneous information, from what I can tell."

"I'll sort those out at some point." Jack slumped back in his chair and rubbed his hands over his face. "This is not how I expected to spend my Saturday."

"So you've said about five times since we got here." Mark crossed the room and put the papers on the desk. Then he kissed Jack's head. "The quicker we get this sorted, the quicker we can get back. It's certainly helping me keep awake. You've given me something to do."

"This is not what I had in mind to stop you succumbing to a concussion."

Mark grinned and sat on the edge of the desk.

"Well, it's working."

Jack rolled his eyes.

"You're impossible, do you know that?"

"I know." Mark's smile faded. "Do you know which one of your parolees could've done this? Anyone stand out in particular?"

"Any of them, but the fact Lucas Banfield's file is the only one that's missing points me to a very specific suspect pool." Jack groaned when something popped up in his head. "Fuck, why did I forget that?"

"What?"

"Denise Banfield works in IT. She's the one below the head of the department."

Mark raised his eyebrows.

"So, a crazy woman in charge of technology to a high level. Great combination, I must say."

"Don't, I'm already feeling bad enough that this has happened."

Denise would have been able to get past the security Jack had and get into the computer. That would be easy for her. But would she be able to get through the extras?

The backup drive. Jack sat forward and his fingers flew across the keys as he brought up the backup drive. Nobody had tried to get into it, and there were no signs of hacking from other computers. He heaved a sigh of relief.

"Thank God for that."

"What?" Mark slid off the desk and came around to lean over the back of his chair. "What is it?"

"I have a backup drive that automatically saves everything. It's currently off-site, but I can access it from here." Jack pointed at the icon on the screen. "I have it disguised as my calendar so it's not immediately visible. It looks like Denise ignored my diary in lieu of getting her son's files deleted."

"Does it have everything on it?"

"Yep. Doesn't matter if something gets deleted off this computer, it doesn't affect the backup. You have to actively get into it and use a specific password to delete the files for good."

Mark made an appreciative noise.

"Nice. And where's the actual backup if someone tried to physically destroy it?"

"At my place."

After having a few dangerous convicts attempt to get into his office and delete some files at the start of his career, Jack had taken extra precautions. You could never be too careful when dealing with people who had been in prison. Even the most placid of people would do something desperate. Jack had never understood why they would do that as it became public record, but it was like they thought if they could get rid of something in their file then their problems would be solved.

Not all criminals were smart, but Jack wasn't about to get through a headache of redoing the work.

"Can you prove who deleted the files?" Mark asked.

"Not on my computer." Jack pointed at the bookcase against the opposite wall. "But I can from the camera footage in this room. I have a tiny camera pointed at the desk. Unless you're actively looking for it, you wouldn't realize that there is a tiny camera tucked into a false book. And that hasn't been moved."

Mark whistled.

"Damn. Listening to all this makes you sound paranoid. And I'm damn glad about that."

"I'd rather be paranoid than lower my guard." Jack grunted. "You'd be surprised how many convicts want to get a piece of me and then claim they were elsewhere."

Mark shuddered.

"And I thought my job was bad."

"You just deal with the criminals in a different capacity, remember?" Jack rose to his feet and crossed the room to pluck the fake book out of the bookcase. "I mostly deal with them long after the fact."

Mark grunted. He straightened up and approached him.

"If it was Denise Banfield who broke in here to delete computer files, she was smart enough to wear gloves or not leave her fingerprints anywhere." He stopped before Jack. "Was it tampered with?"

"From the look of it, no." Jack opened the book and checked the camera. It looked fine. "She wasn't smart enough to think about all the extra bits, from the look of it."

"Have you ever heard of an expression 'you're so smart you're stupid'?"

"Not really." Jack shook his head. "But it makes sense. It's going to take a while to upload everything on this. I need my laptop at home."

"Then we can head home once we've got everything else sorted here." Mark ran a hand through his hair with a yawn. "That file is more likely shredded beyond recognition or gone for good. Physically, at least. Are you going to tell the cops about this? I can call Rusty."

"I want to look at the camera first."

Mark frowned.

"Why didn't you tell the cops about this camera when they were here?"

Jack tried to look innocent.

"I only just remembered when we were talking about security."

He didn't think he succeeded but Mark's expression said he didn't believe him. Mark folded his arms.

"I know you've had bad experiences with the cops, but they're not all bad."

"They're decent enough when you're dealing with children. Everyone will drop everything for children. But not reformed criminals." Jack shrugged. "Most cops think these guys need to stay inside for good."

"And what do you think?"

"Some deserve a second chance. Not all of them, and I do worry that they're going to ignore what they've been told to toe the line, but there are instances when you need to give those who are eager to get back into society a chance."

Again, Mark's expression said he didn't agree on that. Jack knew this was going to be a bone of contention between the two of them, and they wouldn't always see eye-to-eye. Would they be able to get past that to attempt anything beyond what they had?

Damn right you can. If Mark disagrees but accepts what you do, then you're good. If he can't, he's gone.

Jack silently hoped that Mark would understand. He had done so as a friend, but as a lover? That was something else.

It still felt strange addressing Mark as a lover. Was he a boyfriend? Nothing had been said about it, so Jack felt like he was in limbo. He wished he knew what was really going on. When they got back to Mark's place, Jack was going to have it out with him.

He wanted to know where he stood. Mark was open and honest enough to tell him the truth. Jack did not do one-night stands, and he didn't think Mark was the type to do that, either.

Fingers crossed, they were on the same page.

"Jack?" Mark's fingers brushed across Jack's cheek. "You okay? You look like you checked out there."

"Oh. Right. I'm okay." Jack closed his eyes for a brief moment. "I'm just fed up right now. It seems every time I start having a good time, something happens to bring the mood right now. It's almost like someone is watching me and hoping to piss me off." He opened his eyes. "Does that sound selfish?"

Mark's expression softened.

"It's not. With our jobs, it's bound to happen. It's not good, but we have to put up with it because we love our jobs regardless. We're damn good at them."

"Still wish I could deal with decent human beings at times." Jack muttered.

"Would you change your job?"

"Hell, no."

"There you are, then. You're going to have to grit your teeth and get on with it." Mark tugged his head down and kissed him. "But I'll be around for you if you need someone to lean on. If you want me to be there."

"Do you want to be there?"

Jack began to feel hopeful. Maybe this day would turn out okay, after all. Mark wasn't going to leave him to deal with this on his own. For the first time in years, Jack wanted to be able to lean on someone. He didn't want to focus on this alone; he had a habit of internalizing his frustrations, and it manifested in a bad way. Having Mark there, the guy who was level-headed and patient, would be welcoming.

"I want to be there." Mark smiled. "Just give me the word, and I won't be going anywhere."

That sounded like music to Jack's ears. He accepted Mark's kiss, fumbling to put the book on the shelf behind him so he could grab Mark. Mark's body was hard and warm, very warm. Jack couldn't wait to get Mark back into bed.

Or maybe on the couch, it was closer...

A ringing tone had Mark stiffening before pulling away with a groan.

"I'd better get that."

"I know."

That was going to be something they would both need to get used to - having their cell phones going off at practically any time. Jack with parolees complaining or fussing over something and Mark with complaints or kids needing to talk with someone. Mark saw himself as a child advocate and wanted to be there if a child wanted to talk to someone. He put himself out there for all the children, which Jack found admirable.

It was a wonder Mark hadn't broken down already.

Mark frowned as he fished out his cell phone. Then his expression softened when he saw the caller ID.

"It's Mom." Then he groaned. "Shit, I forgot to call and say goodnight to the kids last night."

"They'll understand if you didn't."

"I hope so, otherwise this is Christy calling to tell me off." Mark answered the call. "Hello? Hi, Mom. Are the...?" Then he froze, his voice dying away. Jack saw his face pale. "What? Where is she now? Shit!" The cursing had Jack jumping. "Don't let her in and call the cops when she comes back. I'll be there as soon as I can."

His hand was shaking as he hung up.

"What's happened?"

"Tracey turned up at Mom's house." Mark looked up. He looked scared. "Mom says she was screaming and raving about me ruining her life. She was also brandishing a knife, claiming she would make sure I didn't have kids, either."

Jack went cold. Shit, Tracey Banfield had gone off the deep end.

"How did she even know where your mother lived?"

"I have no idea. But I need to get over there."

Jack didn't even need to think about it. He grabbed Mark's head and kissed him.

"Go. I'll finish off here. You focus on your family."

Mark nodded grimly and hurried from the room. Jack debated shouting after him to be careful, but decided against it. Mark would obviously be careful. He didn't need to worry.

Not much, anyway.

***

Mark was trying not to panic as he drove toward his mother's house. At least his car was still in the parking lot from the night before - Mark's intention to drive it back once Jack's office had been sorted - so he didn't need to pace around waiting for a cab. And Mark didn't feel like putting this on Jack's shoulders, not when he had something serious to focus on himself.

He hoped that Tracey was long gone by the time he got there. He didn't want to deal with the woman trying to threaten his mother and children. Amber had never met Tracey, had never done anything wrong to her. And Stevie and Christy were just children. As a mother herself, what part of Tracey's mind thought it was a good idea to threaten to kill children? Aside from the fact it was going to get her arrested, the moral part of her had to know this was crossing the line in more ways than one.

Then again, various people around her, as well as his own experiences with her, had witnessed a decline in Tracey's attitude and behavior. It seemed to be reducing her reasoning and rationality. Whatever she was taking or whatever was happening to her was making things even worse. After a few calls to Joe and his new partner Alex - briefly Tracey's former attorney - Mark found that they had been getting some phone calls from Tracey and her mother, mostly Joe. They screamed at him for ruining their lives and turning everything upside-down. Mark checked his own messages and found several text messages from Tracey and a few from Denise. They were pretty much accusing him of the same thing.

But why was Tracey at his house and not Joe's? Why was she targeting him instead of her ex-husband?

Mark could only hope that Tracey was still rational enough for him to talk to her and get her to leave or check into a psych ward. She couldn't be in her right mind if she were doing this.

Mark pulled up outside his mother's house to find that there was nobody outside. A couple of flowerpots on the drive had been knocked over, pottery and soil all over the tarmac, and some tire marks on the grass. Tracey had been here, but she wasn't anymore.

Parking behind his mother's car, Mark hurried up to the front door. His brother would have been called and would be on the lookout for Tracey. Mark had agreed to that with Rusty while he was driving over. Mark was to check on the kids and their mother while Rusty looked for Tracey in the usual places. She was getting out of control.

Amber opened the door on the first ring of the doorbell. She was pale and almost burst into tears when she saw Mark.

"Mark! Thank God!"

"Mom." Mark hugged her tightly before gently pushing her in and shutting the door, putting the lock on. "Where are Stevie and Christy?"

"We're here."

Stevie appeared at the top of the stairs. He looked nervous. Mark went to the stairs.

"You okay, buddy?"

"Just freaked out." Stevie gestured down the hallway. "Christy's still hiding in her room. I've put the TV on and turned it up loud so she doesn't have to hear it."

"Good." Mark went up the stairs, kneeling on the steps to be eye-level with the teenage boy. "You're doing good, Stevie."

Stevie nodded. Then he began to shake.

"I don't feel like I'm doing good. When Grandma told us to go upstairs after someone started screaming, I thought she was going to get in. I thought…"

"I know." Mark wrapped his arms around the boy and hugged him. "I know. You're doing great."

Stevie sniffled, his arms tightening around Mark. The kid was terrified. If Mark had witnessed it first-hand, he would more likely feel the same. Stevie and Christy did not need this. Mark could only imagine what horrible memories this was bringing up right now.

Wait a minute, did Stevie just call Amber 'Grandma'?

"Oh, God."

Mark drew back and looked down the stairs. Amber was looking at her cell phone, her eyes wide.

"Mom?" Mark turned to Stevie. "Go into Christy's room and wait there. We'll let you know when you can come out."

"You'll be okay?"

Mark ruffled his hair. Another six months and he wouldn't be able to do that.

"I'll be fine. Go to Christy."

Stevie hurried off and Mark came down the stairs. Amber looked up and turned her cell phone to face him. Mark had almost forgotten about the cameras he and Rusty had put up outside, all accessed by Amber's phone. Taking the phone, Mark watched as someone pulled a car up onto Amber's front lawn and the driver's door opened. Tracey got out, and Mark saw the flash of a knife in her hand. It was one of those big kitchen knives with a wide blade. Mark felt a shiver down his spine. From the way Tracey was screaming and swaying about the lawn, kicking over one of Amber's garden gnomes, she was either very high or very drunk.

Just what they needed now. Mark was beginning to wish he had brought Jack with him; he could knock Tracey over just by breathing on her.

"Get out of there, you stupid bitch!" Tracey's scream was audible through the door and on the cell phone. "Tell me where the bastard is! Where the fuck is he?"

"She did the same thing earlier." Amber whispered. "But she stopped on the drive last time. I told her to go away, I didn't open the door, and then she got the knife out and threatened to barge her way in."

"Did you tell her you were calling the cops?"

"I did, and I have. They're on their way." Amber flinched as something hard hit the door. "Who the hell is she?"

"She's Joe Swarbrick's ex-wife."

Mark didn't talk about his cases with his mother - he liked to keep confidentiality if he could - but Amber knew Joe. They had met a handful of times, and Amber liked Joe. The feeling was mutual. She

111

knew enough of the story from him without Mark needing to say anything.

Amber's eyes widened.

"That's the ex-wife? How did Joe manage to have a family with someone as crazy as that?"

"I'm sure she wasn't always crazy."

"She must've been. You don't go from zero to a hundred out of nowhere." Amber shook her head. "She must've been very good at hiding the crazy."

And distance from her family helped. Mark was still under the impression that Denise and Lucas Banfield were the reason Tracey was slipping fast now. She had been a good person and fantastic mother when they lived elsewhere with limited contact, but now they were in the same area, it was like a different person. They had to be the catalyst for all of this.

Another thud made the door rattle. From the look of it on the cameras, Tracey was kicking the door. Mark was not having this. If Tracey got in before the cops got there, she was going to go after his mother and children.

"Call the cops again and let them know she has come back. I'm going out the back door."

"What?" Amber looked horrified. "You're not going to confront her, are you?"

"Would you rather she comes in and you shoot her?" Mark headed towards the back of the house. "Just let the cops know she's back, Mom!"

Letting himself out of the kitchen door, Mark jogged around to the front of the house. Tracey was still hitting the door with her fist, her other hand clenched tightly around the knife. Mark felt a moment of panic. He hadn't talked down anyone holding a knife. What was he doing?

Protecting your family, that's what you're doing.

"Tell me where the bastard is!" Tracey screamed, kicking the door. "He ruined my life! Now I'm going to ruin his!"

How was this not bringing out the neighbors? This was a nosy area, and people were always sticking their heads out to see what was going on. Mark had seen his mother's neighbors hovering around in their front lawns pretending to garden or wash their cars when it wasn't needed just so they could have something to gossip about. Decent people, but that habit was annoying.

Mark wished that annoying habit would rear its head right now. He had a feeling he was going to need it.

He approached Tracey as Tracey gave the front door a running kick. This time the wood cracked and the doorframe itself started rattling. She kept this up, and she was going to kick the door down.

"Tracey!" Mark grabbed her arm and hauled her away. "What the hell are you doing?"

Tracey screamed and swung the knife. Mark let go and jumped back, the blade missing his stomach. Tracey's eyes were wild, and her pupils were so large that Mark couldn't see the color. She was very high on something. Tracey bared her teeth and brandished the knife at him.

"You! You bastard!"

"What the hell do you think you're doing?" Mark tensed, ready to either run if Tracey charged or grab at the knife. "How did you find out where I live?"

"Mom's good with computers. She found out your address with just a few clicks of the mouse." Tracey was breathing heavily. "She said you don't deserve to be a father, not after what you've done. And I agree."

"What have I done?"

"You ruined my life, and my family's. Mom is so distraught she can't get out of bed. We did nothing to deserve it."

She was on something very strong if it was screwing up the rational part of her. Anyone with common sense wouldn't bring their children around a sex offender, even if they had a familial bond. If Tracey were level-headed, she would understand. Denise and Lucas had done a number on her.

She was incredibly lucky Lily and James had been seen by doctors since that declaration and both said neither had been touched in a way that would make them uncomfortable. Or she would be in hot water as well.

Mark eyed the knife, which was shaking in her tight grip.

"You put your children in a dangerous situation, Tracey."

"My brother..."

"Is a convicted sex offender and he's not supposed to be around children. This has been told to you multiple times. You also reported your ex-husband for false child abuse claims, which is going to be marked down for you. I was just doing my job and keeping children safe. Your children."

Tracey snorted.

"Your job? That's a joke! Your job is to bring misery to people. You've been doing this to me for years!"

Mark frowned. Years? He had only known Tracey Banfield and her situation for the last six months.

"Years? What are you...?"

"I loved you, Joe!" Tracey wailed. "And I put up with your tantrums about my family because I loved you. You said they were trash and bad for me, that I was better without that. They were never trash. That would be you!"

That was when realization dawned. Tracey was too far gone in her delusions. Whatever she was taking had skewed everything in her head. Was she actually seeing her ex-husband in front of her or was she seeing him? Mark held up his hands and started to move closer to her.

"Tracey, my name's not Joe. I'm not your ex-husband. I'm Mark, remember?"

Tracey shook her head.

"Don't lie to me, Joe. You've lied to me long enough!"

"I'm Mark Washington, your CPS worker. You're at my mother's house threatening my mother and my children with a knife." Mark wanted to shout, but he didn't think that was going to get through. "You need to put the knife down and step away from it. Otherwise, you're going to hurt yourself and others. You don't want to hurt anyone, do you?"

"You think I'm not going to use it!" Tracey jabbed the knife at him. "You think I'm a weakling. I've never been a weakling, Joe, and I'm going to prove it."

"I'm not your ex-husband, Tracey." Mark was close enough to reach out and grab the knife. "Please, just put the knife down. Then we can talk about this."

For a moment, he thought Tracey was going to put the knife aside and actually do as she was told. There was a flicker in her eyes, which Mark hoped was her saying she was hearing him. Then he heard the sirens. And they were getting closer. Thank God, the cavalry was here now.

That was like flicking a switch in Tracey's head. Her eyes narrowed and she snarled. As Mark reached for the knife, Tracey yanked her hand back. Mark missed the handle, his fingers closing around the blade. Pain flashed through his hand as Tracey drew the blade over his fingers, and then Tracey lunged at him. Mark grabbed at her, his injured hand going around her wrist, but his feet went out from under him as Tracey's legs tangled with his. They fell over, landing hard on the grass. Mark's head bounced off the lawn hard enough for him to see stars. Something sharp stabbed him in the small of his back, and then he was aware of the white-hot pain in his chest. Tracey was sitting up, her eyes widening in horror as she stared at the knife sticking out of Mark's chest.

Mark was aware of her getting off him, but she was getting blurry as she scrambled away. Someone was screaming. Mark wasn't sure who was screaming. Things were turning into white noise in his head, everything going black.

The last thing he remembered was someone touching his face and someone begging him to wake up.

Chapter Eight

He should have been there. Jack was still shaking two hours after being told about Mark's accident. He should have been there with him to make sure Mark had backup. But he hadn't, and Mark had gotten stabbed. The doctors were optimistic that he would be fine as the knife had penetrated nearer his shoulder than his heart and hadn't nicked any vital organs, but that didn't make Jack feel any better.

He just felt incredibly cold when Rusty called him to give him the situation. Jack barely remembered getting to the hospital, or the wait in the waiting room while Mark was in surgery. Amber and the kids had been there, all of them ashen-faced. Amber was hugging Christy, who was sobbing into her arms until she ended up falling asleep, and Stevie had been standing in a corner, hunched over and staring at the floor. He refused to interact with anyone until Jack went to him and touched his shoulder. Then Stevie was throwing himself into Jack's arms, sobbing louder than his sister.

They had seen their foster father lying there with a knife sticking out his chest. Jack's heart broke for them. And for Amber, who looked close to snapping. She had been helping her son out, and she had almost witnessed him get killed.

Rusty told Jack that Tracey had been detained by some neighbors, who had actually witnessed the attack. She tried to fight back but was tackled pretty quickly. Now she was in custody where they were determining if she needed to be in the cells or in a psych ward. Jack hoped the latter and they made sure she never got out.

He could hardly believe that Tracey had actually been a decent person at some point. Not after what she had done. And when she had been raised by a woman enmeshed with her son and condoned his criminal actions, it was no surprise that Tracey had turned out the way she had.

But did she have to stab someone who was actually trying to get them all help? What part of that thought it was a good idea? Jack wouldn't be surprised if it came back that Denise had been pouring lies into Tracey's ears before doping her up and sending her on her way. It was like she didn't truly care about Tracey, just got her to do the dirty jobs.

At least they had something on Denise. Jack had handed the camera from his office to Rusty, and Mark's brother promised he would look at it as soon as he could. He wanted to be there for his brother, but Jack said he would be better off making sure Mark's attacker was dealt with. Rusty was more tightly wound than Amber, and Jack didn't want Rusty's temper to let loose with children around. The older brother was out for blood.

Join the queue, mate.

It felt like hours before he got news, although not the news Jack really wanted. Rusty texted him to say he had looked at the footage and it was definitely Denise who had broken into his office. She had gone through all the files, throwing them around when she was done. At one point it looked like it was snowing. Then she put what Jack guessed was Lucas' file into the shredder before putting the shredded paper into her handbag and getting onto the computer. Jack had been able to check his backup drive, and it was still okay. No one had attempted to get into it from another computer. If Denise had found out about it, she hadn't started on it yet.

That was something, but Jack hoped they could get hold of her first. She was not at home and wasn't turning up anywhere. Rusty said Denise had just vanished.

The woman was turning into more of a psychopath than Jack expected. He had always thought she was a little weird and little too obsessed with her son. She had been staunchly on his side from day one, even when Jack said the best thing she could do was step back and let Lucas deal with it on his own. She just would not let him do things of his own volition. Even when Lucas was speaking, he looked to his mother. If Jack hadn't known their relationship, he would have thought they were husband and wife.

That made him feel sick. Jack had seen parents obsessed with children like this before, and it still made him uncomfortable.

It was no wonder Lucas barely knew how to behave and live like a grown man if he had spent his childhood with Denise Banfield and then the majority of his adult life in jail.

It felt like forever when the doctor came to find them to let them know Mark was out and in his room recovering. Amber had started to cry then, with Stevie and Christy hugging her. Jack had felt the weight come off his shoulders so fast he had to sit down before he fell over. At least Mark was going to be okay. He would be in hospital for a few days and then told to rest at home, but he was alive. Jack didn't think he would be able to cope if Mark had died and he wasn't there.

Amber was still in a mess, everything finally piling down on her, so when the doctor said they could go and see Mark she managed to stutter out that Jack could go and see Mark first. They would be along when she was calmer. Stevie nodded in agreement, while Christy just held on tighter to Amber. Jack's heart ached at the sight. The two kids had lost their parents in such a horrible way and had been building up with someone new, a new father to them, and they had almost lost him as well.

Jack wasn't sure how he managed to get to Mark's room when everything felt like he was walking through treacle, but he managed somehow. And the sight of Mark lying half-propped up on his bed, awake but pale, threatened to have him crying as well. To Jack, Mark was a strong person. He was more than capable of looking after himself, so to see him like this, his chest bandaged up as well as his hand, was frightening.

Shit. He almost lost Mark when they had barely gotten started.

Mark looked around as Jack stood frozen in the doorway, the nurse checking his vitals on the machine. He managed a slight smile in Jack's direction.

"Don't look at me like that. I'm okay. It was just a flesh wound."

"You..." Jack stared. "Just a flesh wound? You were stabbed in the fucking chest, Mark! You could've been killed!"

"But I'm fine. I'm alive. See?"

Mark held up his hand, the one not with bandages around his fingers. Jack growled.

"That doesn't make me feel any better, Mark."

The nurse glanced between them.

"Do you need a few minutes alone? I can do these vitals later."

"If you don't mind?" Mark didn't take his eyes off Jack. "Just a couple of minutes."

"All right." The nurse headed towards the door, nodding at Jack as she passed him. "Buzz me in when you're done."

She left, closing the door behind her. It was then that Jack was able to move. He didn't know when he walked into the room and saw Mark in that state whether to kiss him or throttle him. He had to know that trying to get a knife off a crazy person was not going to go well.

But in the few quick strides he made to the bed with Mark reaching for him, Jack went for the former, cupping Mark's head to kiss him hard. Mark flinched and writhed away.

"Careful! My injuries!"

"Sorry." Jack brushed his fingers over Mark's shoulder, avoiding the obvious lump where the thick bundle of bandage was over the wound. "How does it feel?"

"Burns." Mark grimaced. "Hurt like hell at the time. I'm just glad I came around from surgery quickly."

"You don't feel any after-effects?"

"Not massively. Just a bit sluggish. That stuff wears off pretty quickly, so they had to keep on top of it while stitching me up or I would've been conscious. Not fun to know I could've been awake during surgery." Mark pressed his hand to his wound and winced. "Fuck, I never thought it would be like that."

"Shit, Mark." Jack rested his forehead against Mark's. "I won't lie, when Rusty called me, I was scared. I was scared you were going to die."

"I thought the same as well." Mark cupped Jack's jaw, brushing a kiss over his mouth. "But don't worry about me, Jack."

"How can I not worry when you're like this? You got a concussion yesterday and then you get stabbed today. How am I supposed to sit back and be okay with this?"

"That came out wrong." Mark drew back and managed a smile. "Look, I'm alive. My hand and chest are burning, but I'm awake and the doctors are optimistic that I'm going to be okay. It's going to take more than what happened to me to knock me down."

Jack groaned.

"Don't say that, please! Or the next thing that happens to you will be more drastic."

"How can you get more drastic than someone stabbing me?"

"Do you want me to go through that?"

Mark shook his head and closed his eyes.

"Perhaps not."

He didn't look like the confident man Jack had met, known and fallen for. He looked scared. Very scared.

Hang on, did he just say that he had fallen for Mark?

Yes, you did.

The knowledge of that was more grounding than Jack expected. He loved Mark, and while he didn't appreciate finding out just as he was close to losing the guy, he was glad it had come out. At least, come out to himself. It was going to take a bit more courage to tell Mark, and now wasn't really the time.

You played strip monopoly last night to get him naked and into bed and you're backing out on telling him you love him now?

"Where's Tracey now? Has she been dealt with?"

"In a sense." Jack had spoken to Rusty about it earlier. He couldn't remember much about the last few hours, but he did remember that. "She's been arrested for criminal damage and felony assault."

"Not attempted murder?"

"You need premeditation for that."

Mark snorted.

"Like hell. She went there with a knife and threatened to ruin my life. She had intent for that."

"I'll speak to Rusty about it." Jack sat on the edge of the bed, resting Mark's injured hand in his lap and absently stroking the back of Mark's hand. "She went even crazier in the cells, so she's been prepared to send off to the psych ward. Rusty thinks she had a mental break exacerbated by drugs."

"Drugs." Mark closed his eyes for a second before opening them again. "I suspected she was on them when I saw her. Is it possible to have a mental breakdown due to drug abuse?"

"Highly possible." Jack frowned. "I thought you knew about drug use."

123

"Do I?" Mark frowned. "I think my concussion was made worse. I hit the grass pretty hard."

"You should've said something."

"As long as I don't get up from this bed and walk around, I'll be fine. This is as much as I can manage right now." Mark swallowed. "Can I have some water? My throat's really dry."

"Sure."

Jack reached for the jug of water on the table at the foot of Mark's bed and poured out a glass. He held it for Mark as Mark took slow, careful sips. It was surreal to see Mark like this. Jack hoped it wasn't a temporary thing; it was making his nerves fray. Mark could have died. He was extremely lucky that the knife hadn't been a couple of inches closer. He put the glass down and turned back to Mark.

"Rusty says they're going to run a tox screen on her when she's in hospital, but they're confident it's one of those drugs that can make you hallucinate pretty badly."

"That would be almost any of them. Tracey kept looking at me and calling me Joe." Mark shook his head. "She must've thought she was somehow at Joe's place and her head turned things around."

"Rusty said he would get hold of Joe to make him aware. They're doing okay, apparently, although Joe is rather shaken."

It was hardly a surprise; Joe and Tracey had been married for a while and they had been great until Tracey changed in recent years. Even with the resentment and anger, it was difficult not to turn off how you cared about someone you had been with for several years. Jack understood that. He was glad no one else had been hurt.

He just wished no one had been hurt.

"This is such a mess." Mark rubbed a hand over his eyes. "Joe said Tracey never took drugs with him. She was adamant about drink and drugs, said she wouldn't allow them near the kids. Then they moved back to the area and things changed drastically."

"When was this?"

"About the same time Lucas got out of jail." Mark blinked. "You think those two things are connected?"

"They have to be." Jack said grimly. "Lucas was always a bad influence. Joe had been told that by Tracey many times when they lived in another state. Why she would go back to hell after leaving it and getting clean, Joe had no idea. But he thought they could foster something relatively decent."

Sweet summer child, Jack's mother would call him. Hoping for the best, and it never really happened. Joe was now divorced but thankfully had custody of his children and a partner Jack was sure was going to be a permanent fixture. From what he heard, the attraction between the two men was pretty much electric from the get-go, and something like that didn't die down so quickly. At least Lily and James were out of it now. Jack didn't want to think what could have happened if Tracey had majority custody.

"Let's hope we get some answers from her once she's come down from her high." Mark grunted.

"From the way she was with the neighbors and the cops, I have a feeling that might be a while."

125

"I'm going to be laid up for a while as well. I think I can handle it. Speaking of crazy people, did you find out if it was Denise Banfield who broke into your office?"

"Yes, Rusty told me. I was on my way to take it to the cops when he called me about..." Jack cleared his throat. "He looked over it for me. It was definitely her. With the audio as well, you can hear her muttering to herself. Mostly profanities directed at me."

It was a shame they hadn't gotten any fingerprints, but the hidden camera gave the cops more than enough evidence to charge Denise once they got hold of her. Jack knew Rusty was a little salty that Jack hadn't handed the camera over at the time the cops were combing through for evidence, but Jack could claim he forgot. In a sense, he had.

That and after the times the cops had made things difficult for him in the past, Jack decided to be awkward towards them. Childish, yes, but Jack felt like being childish at times. Rusty would have to deal with it if Jack was going to be dating Mark.

Dating Mark. That did sound good.

"Do you know if they've arrested her yet?" Mark asked.

"No, but from what Rusty said, she wasn't at her house and not in her usual places. Her parents don't know where she is and haven't heard from her since their grandson went back into jail. They tried asking Lucas, but Lucas gave them a lot of expletives and threats. Guy's been put into isolation because he's been picking fights with everyone and it was for his own safety."

"Charming."

"God, you have no idea."

Mark grunted. Then he yawned and rubbed his eyes. At least he was getting some color back into his cheeks.

"So, where do you think we'll start?"

Jack stared.

"'We'? What's this 'we'? You're going to stay in the hospital until the doctors say you can go home, and even then you'll be in bed."

"What?" Mark began to sit up, flinching sharply. "Not fair!"

"Yes, fair." Jack pressed a hand to Mark's good shoulder and eased him back down. "You've been through too much the last couple of days. It's a wonder you're still conscious. And you really think you're going to do anything when you've got an IV inserted? I'd like to see you get that out without any help."

Mark looked down and his face paled even more as he was reminded that he had an IV needle inserted into the back of his hand. Jack knew Mark hated needles and would avoid them if he possibly could. There was no way he was going to get up and walk around if he had that thing in; nobody would do that until Mark didn't need it, and Mark knew it. The fact he had bounced back to sharp consciousness so quickly was nothing short of a miracle.

Jack didn't want that to be undone by Mark getting up and doing something stupid.

"Look, Mark, you need to stay in here and let the doctors look after you. It's the best course of action for you."

Mark scowled. He was beginning to look like a pouting kid.

"I hate missing out on the fun."

Jack snorted.

"If you think this is fun, you hit your head harder than I thought."

"It's certainly more fun than me sitting here with only a crappy TV for company."

"You can go without the infinite channels and YouTube for a while long." Jack chuckled. "But I can bring in your laptop tomorrow, if you want."

"Please. I need something to stop me from going mad."

"Well, getting plenty of rest is something you should be doing. I'm sure you're going to crash in a while." Jack glanced towards the door. "Your mom and kids are in the waiting room. Do you want to see them?"

"I..." Mark bit his lip. "I'm not sure I want them to see me like this."

"Mark, you scared them. Christy hasn't stopped crying, and Amber's only just breaking down. It would make them feel better knowing that you're okay."

Mark looked like he wanted to argue, but he sighed and nodded.

"Okay. I think it will make me feel better. Did they get hurt?"

"Not at all. They were safe." Jack leaned over and kissed him. "I'll be around if you need me."

"Always." Mark managed a smile. "That's a given."

That made Jack feel better than he did when he first entered the room.

***

Mark was glad he was not being prodded and poked anymore. He had been knocked out but still aware enough to feel the surgeons poking around and sewing up his wounds. That had hurt like a bitch, but Mark had been paralyzed to pull away. If he'd known that stuff wouldn't actually knock him out, he would have asked for a higher dose.

His threshold for knock-out gas seemed to be far higher than he expected.

It hurt like hell even lying on the bed. His shoulder was burning and his lower back had also been stitched up. Mark had fallen onto some of the broken flowerpot pieces, and a shard had stabbed him in the back, narrowly missing his kidney. Mark was incredibly lucky on both counts, and he had been looked after well enough, but it didn't make the pain go away. Morphine wasn't cutting it. Mark could feel every single stitch they had put in. It felt like he could rip his skin if he shifted a little too much.

Mark hated being immobile unless he was sleeping, so to lie in a hospital bed until deemed well enough to go home was going to be a nightmare for him. Mark didn't even slow down when he had the flu, which just made him even worse. Amber had told him off many times for not focusing on his own health.

His mother was still shaking even as she left the room, somewhat relieved that her son was alive. Stevie and Christy had run into the room in front of Amber, both of them flinging themselves onto Mark. That had hurt Mark's shoulder and he felt like the IV was ripping out of his hand, but he couldn't bring himself to be upset. He was just glad to see the two of them were okay. Stevie buried his head on Mark's shoulder quietly sobbing, while Christy curled up on his lap. Amber simply kissed Mark's head and stroked his hair, her eyes shimmering with fresh tears. It killed him to see his mother, normally such a strong woman, look so frightened.

You didn't go out there to get stabbed. You went to make a maniac calm down. If there's anyone to blame, it's Tracey Banfield.

A woman who was going to be in a psych ward for a while, most likely detoxing. Joe had suspected that Tracey was on drugs, and she had been court-ordered to go into rehab. If Tracey had done as she was told, things might have been different now. But her mother had gotten her claws into her daughter and turned her into a person that her own children wouldn't recognize.

Denise Banfield was starting to show her real face. She was also showing that she would do anything for her son while letting her daughter flounder without a life preserver. Mark really wouldn't be surprised if Denise had encouraged her son to feed his sister drugs to keep her compliant and dependent, to the detriment of her own child. Or children. Lucas was a victim of Denise's enmeshment, although Mark couldn't see a man like him as a victim. Not much. Denise had started all this, and it had gotten out of control.

This should have happened a long time ago. Tracey should have stayed away. Lucas should have stayed in jail.

But then you wouldn't have met Jack, would you?

130

That was a point, although Mark didn't want to credit someone else's misery for meeting the man he had fallen in love with.

Love. He loved Jack. That didn't scare Mark to say it to himself as much as he thought. And Jack was still there while his kids and Amber stayed, hovering in the doorway while his family prodded him to make sure he was still alive. When Mark caught his eye, Jack gave him a slight smile and a nod. He wasn't going anywhere.

Mark didn't want his kids to go, but visiting hours were over and they needed to get home. Amber was going to watch over them in Mark's house after what happened at hers, which everyone agreed was the best idea. Christy had given Mark a hard hug before sliding off the bed, calling him something that had Mark freezing.

She called him Dad.

Dad. She had never done that before. And it rolled off the tongue so easily. Before Mark could recover himself, Stevie had said bye and left, also calling him Dad. From the look on Amber's face, she knew it was happening. She kissed her startled son's head before following the children, leaving Mark still shocked. The kids had never been pressured to call him 'Dad', and Mark said they could call him whatever they wanted. They had never asked to call him 'Dad'.

And Mark liked it. Very much so. It made him feel better knowing that there were people who wanted him as their family. Mark had wanted a family of his own, and he wanted to make a difference with kids. From the way Stevie and Christy had been recently, being very mature kids, Mark liked to think he had done that.

Jack left shortly after Mark's family, promising to come back later with his laptop and a few things. Mark didn't think he could get back onto the ward, but Jack had a glint in his eye when he said he would find a way. Knowing the guy, he would.

It took a while for Mark to get settled. He was exhausted and his head was hurting more than his shoulder and back, so sleep was not going to come for a while. The nurses would only give him a limited amount of pain relief, and it didn't seem to be enough. Mark hated it. He just wanted to be knocked out and let things sort themselves out while he lay unconscious. No such luck, sadly. He was lying there, feeling all the stitches and pretty sure that there were a few dents in his head.

At least there was something relatively decent on the TV. Mark watched a baseball game and then a black-and-white movie. It was mundane but fun at the same time. Not something that would keep him awake but something to vaguely focus on.

Afternoon turned into evening. Jack had said he would be along later on, so Mark wanted to stay awake to see him again. Maybe have a bit of a makeout session, if Jack was up for it. Mark couldn't really do anything, hooked up as he was, but he was happy to make Jack leave with a smile on his face. In spite of everything, Mark was feeling very daring.

But sleep overcame his desire to see Jack and Mark found himself closing his eyes. Somehow, he slipped into sleep that had been threatening to arrive but couldn't with the throbbing in his head. Now Mark felt relaxed enough to rest. Jack would wake him up when he got here. Give him a kiss like Sleeping Beauty. Mark almost smiled at the thought. Jack was certainly better looking than Prince Philip.

When Mark was roused, he was aware of someone standing by his bed. For a moment, he thought it was a nurse doing her rounds and checking his IV bag. Then he thought it was Jack, but it didn't feel like his presence. It was a presence that made Mark's body feel cold.

His gut said he had an unwelcome visitor.

Mark opened his eyes, and almost yelled aloud when he saw Denise Banfield leaning over him.

"Jesus!"

"It's okay." Denise held up a hand as Mark tried to figure out how to scramble away when he was stuck in a narrow bed. "Don't panic. I'm not going to hurt you."

"I don't believe you."

Mark's heart was racing. How the hell did she manage to get past all the nurses? Denise wasn't exactly a small woman; she stood out like a sore thumb. He fumbled for the button that would summon the nurses, only for it to be swiped away as he brushed his fingers over it. Denise moved the button to the table out of reach.

"No, Mr. Washington, we won't be doing that. We're going to talk, and I can't do that if you start calling for the nurses like a baby." She sighed and looked him up and down. "I heard my daughter had hurt you, and I wanted to make sure you were okay."

Mark was doing his best not to panic. It was darker, and the time on the clock said people were beginning to settle down for the night. He could only hope that a nurse got here before Denise did anything. Even if he reached for the button, he would either fall out of bed or Denise would hit him. She might have said she wasn't going to hurt him, but Mark didn't believe that at all.

"How the hell did you get in here, Mrs. Banfield?"

"I'm a clever girl. I snuck in." Denise leaned on the bed, leaning over him. "I can do anything once I put my mind to it."

"I don't doubt it." Mark tried to crane away without sliding out of bed. God, he was sure Denise could hear his heart racing. "What are you really doing here?"

"I told you, I came to see how you were."

"Pardon me if I don't believe you."

Denise's eyes flickered. She sighed.

"You don't know what it's like to have a mother's love for a child. A man can't experience love like that."

"I'm a parent, Mrs. Banfield."

Denise snorted and waved a hand.

"Foster parents don't count."

"Oh, really?" Mark gritted his teeth. "Would you like to say that again, because foster parents are a lot more important than you think."

"They're still not real parents. So, they're not going to count in this." Denise looked annoyed that Mark was arguing. "Fathers aren't any better. My husband was an awful parent. He didn't know how to love kids. A mother's love...that is special. And a mother will do anything for their children."

"You came here to tell me that?" Mark gestured at their surroundings. "Wait until I'm unable to get away to say that?"

Denise's expression changed a little. It was marginal, but Mark saw it. And it sent a shiver down his spine.

"I just wanted you to know. You're a man. You won't truly understand these things. If our kids want something, we're the ones who bend over backwards to get it for them. We will protect them from anything."

Mark thought about arguing about his role - hell, he had just been called 'Dad' for the first time - but he guessed that this would have just gone over her head. He glanced at the call button. If it was just a little closer...

"Your son molested children." He said quietly. "How did you protect him from committing a crime in the first place? And your daughter? She tried to get away and got herself clean. Away from you, she knew you were a bad influence."

"But she came back. As she was supposed to do, my weak little bitch." Denise's lip curled. "And then you, Swarbrick and McGuire had to fuck it up. It's always the men who muck things up. I have to put it back together."

"Does that include your son as well?" Mark asked. "Because he certainly fucked things up."

Denise's nostrils flared. She leaned closer, and Mark really wished he could get away. He had never felt more helpless.

"My son is a good boy. He wouldn't hurt anyone."

"He was convicted of felony charges, Mrs. Banfield. He's lucky that he was given parole, given the severity."

"He was an innocent man. The system was up against him in the beginning. Because they had him 'flagged'." She said the last word in a sneer. "It wasn't his fault."

Mark had heard husbands making excuses for their wives regarding abuse and vice versa. This was the first time he heard, out loud, a mother saying that a convicted and dangerous child molester was an innocent man. Jack must hear it all the time, and Mark had no idea how he could not react so much to it.

He stared at Denise, who seemed to be leaning in even closer. Her perfume was tickling his nostril to the point it made him want to sneeze.

"Who gave your daughter drugs?" He whispered. "Was it your son? Or was it you? I mean, you said a mother always does whatever her children want."

There was a slight waver when Mark suggested it was her. Ah, that was an answer. Then it was gone and Denise snorted before pushing away from the bed.

"Like I said, you wouldn't understand."

"Is that why you're here? You came to gloat?"

"No, that was not my intention." Denise began pacing, throwing her hands up in the air. "I came here to tell you to leave us alone. We were doing fine until Tracey married Joe and started getting a conscience. She came back, and things went back to how they were before. As it should be. Then Joe Swarbrick had to get in the way. And you." She spat in his direction. "And McGuire."

Tracey was the scapegoat. But she couldn't have a life of her own. Denise had to control her. So, she had fed Tracey drugs to keep her dependent. Mark shuddered to think how Denise had reacted when Tracey left - how she managed to find a good guy to marry, Mark had no idea - and wondered how long it was before Denise was feeding Tracey drugs again.

Tracey had a lot of problems, but Denise was the root of all of them.

Mark saw a flicker behind Denise. The door was opening very slowly, and Jack was appearing around the door. His expression was set in stone, glowering at Denise's back. Mark caught his eye and shook his head slightly. He didn't need Jack tackling Denise and the two grappling in his room. And if Jack bought out his gun, there was a chance something could go wrong. Jack looked like he was about to go after Denise.

Mark sat up slowly, gingerly shifting the hand with the IV attached. Now was not the time to get squeamish.

"I'll tell you this now, Denise." He was surprised that his voice wasn't shaking. "I know a mother's love. My mother's. She protected me from danger, made sure that I didn't make any bad choices. Sure, I made a few mistakes, but she brought me back on track. And I pass that onto my foster kids. I may not give them the motherly care and affection that they need, but I can be a parent. And I can make sure they can be good people." He sat forward as Denise scoffed. "That's where you and I differ. Somewhere along the line, you and your ideas about love and being there for your children got warped. They weren't good intentions at all. They were about control. About enabling. And you enabled your children to make very bad decisions."

Denise bared her teeth. Mark was sure she had just growled.

"I'm a good mother!" She cried.

"No, you're not." Mark didn't flinch as Denise glowered at him. She looked ready to pounce. "If you were, you would've made sure that Lucas didn't commit a felony crime. That Tracey didn't take drugs. That you wouldn't have brought your grandchildren around a child molester."

Denise's eyes were wild. Had she really thought she could sneak in here and tell him how things were, that she had done nothing wrong? What person in their right mind thought that was a good idea? And she hadn't even noticed Jack moving into the room.

"Family sticks together, Washington!" Denise was now breathing heavily. She had flipped her switch pretty quickly as well. "Always. You wouldn't understand."

"Why? Because I don't have kids of my own?" Mark challenged. He always smarted when people said that. "Just because my foster children aren't blood-related doesn't mean I won't go to hell and back for them."

They glared at each other. Mark knew he was at a slight disadvantage if Denise chose to attack him right now, but he wasn't about to back down. And he was sure, for the most part, that Jack would get there before Denise laid a hand on him.

For a moment, he thought that Denise was going to charge him. She looked angry enough to do it. But instead, her shoulders slumped and she hung

138

her head. Then her body shook. Was she crying? She was switching emotions so much Mark couldn't keep up. He wouldn't be surprised if she were on drugs as well.

"What..." Denise sniffed. "What do I do? I was doing so well, and then it all went to hell. What do I do?"

Mark looked up at Jack.

"You can make it right by getting your kids the help they need. By making sure they don't hurt anyone else. And by turning yourself in to Mr. McGuire. Jack?"

Denise started and spun around to find Jack standing behind her. She stiffened, and Mark thought she was going to lash out. But Denise slumped even more, leaning into Jack as she began to cry. Jack stood there awkwardly with her leaning against his chest. Then he cleared his throat and set her away gently.

"Let's go, Mrs. Banfield." He glanced at Mark. "I'll be along later."

Mark nodded. As long as he did that, Mark didn't care about anything else. He was in too much pain to think about it any further.

Chapter Nine

When Jack had come back with Mark's laptop and a few clothes, he hadn't expected to find Denise Banfield in Mark's room. How had she managed to get in there without any of the staff noticing? They were the type of people who would notice when someone was breathing the wrong way. Denise was a very sneaky woman.

And obviously high. Whatever she had been feeding her daughter she had been taking as well. Her emotions were all over the place, and she could get very agitated with barely any pushing. She tried to hit and kick Jack a few times on the way out to the front of the hospital, even with her hands cuffed behind her. Jack's shin was smarting.

The cops were outside to take her away. Denise would be spending a few nights in jail until someone posted her bail. Jack didn't bet on that happening, seeing as Denise didn't really have anyone to help her out with that. She had burned a lot of bridges, it seemed.

Jack stood on the sidewalk and watched as Denise was taken away. How was it possible that a woman of her age could be such a vile human being? She had turned her son into a felon and her daughter into a dependent drug addict. And she called herself a good mother? Jack couldn't wrap his head around that. Just like he couldn't wrap his head around the fact he had come into Mark's room to find her pacing around like a loon. It was a wonder she hadn't hurt Mark.

When Jack got back to Mark's room, he found his lover being checked over by one of the nurses.

She was putting extra tape over the IV needle and shaking her head when Jack stepped into the room.

"I'm so sorry again, Mr. Washington. I have no idea how she managed to get in like that."

"She didn't hurt me." Mark sounded gentle, surprising considering what had just happened. "And it wouldn't have made any difference. She's a sneaky woman."

"I just know my manager is not going to be happy when she finds out." The nurse looked up at Jack. "Has she gone?"

"She's gone." Jack gave her a smile. "And we're not going to blame anyone here. If she can get into my backyard when the gate is locked, she can get onto a secure hospital unit."

That placated her a little. The nurse straightened up and scribbled a note in Mark's file.

"Well, just as long as it doesn't happen again. Oh, there was a backpack and a gym bag outside the door when I came in. I'm guessing you brought it for Mr. Washington?"

"Yes."

"It's on the couch over there." The nurse nodded at the pullout couch under the window. "I'll leave you to it."

She left, Jack closing the door behind her. Mark let out a huge sigh of relief.

"She was fussing over me like I'd been facing down Michael Myers. I think she was worried I was going to put in a complaint."

"I think you faced Jason and Mrs. Vorhees."

"Very funny." Mark rolled his eyes. "How's Mrs. Banfield? Was she still a blubbering mess?"

"Got a little physical, but nothing I can't handle." Jack crossed the room and sat on the bed. "I'm surprised you had a head after what you said. She looked close to snapping if you so much as sneezed."

"I'm surprised she didn't stab me as I slept." Mark rubbed his chest with a wince. "I had no idea how long she was standing there until I realized someone was in the room. That leaves me cold."

"I know." Jack took his hand and kissed his bandaged fingers. "I'm just glad you're okay."

"Same." Mark sighed, his injured fingers curling around Jack's. "This is going to be a big mess to untangle."

Jack couldn't agree more. Lucas and Tracey might have had a chance of becoming good, decent people if they had had a decent person raising them. Tracey had shown when she was away from their influence that she could be a good person, a loving mother. Now she was unrecognizable. Jack could only hope that she cleaned up in rehab and managed to sort herself out. That influence needed to be broken so she could have a semblance of a relationship with her children.

Normally, Jack would say a woman like that didn't deserve children to know her. But Tracey wasn't bad. She had just been a puppet. Jack was sure they could trace her decline back to when Denise started giving her drugs. They had to be the reason Tracey behaved erratically and like she had a vendetta to settle.

Swarbrick would do the right thing. He would understand.

"Do you think if Denise had been raised decently herself that this wouldn't have happened?" Jack asked. "I suspect not, given her own parents and what happened there."

"Why?" Mark looked interested. "What did happen?"

"Later." Jack leaned in. "Right now, I want to do something else."

He had been thinking nothing else but kissing Mark on the way back to the hospital. That had gone out of his head when he had seen the uninvited guest. But now she was gone, Jack could have what he wanted. Mark accepted the kiss with a sigh, and Jack was sure he was smiling.

"You can do more of that when I get out of here." Mark whispered against his mouth. "Although I might have to be on my back for a while. And you would have to have temporary control over rules in the bedroom."

"Have to have?" Jack started laughing. "You don't want to relinquish that control, do you?"

"Not really."

Jack kissed him again. It was things like that which made him love Mark. He nibbled on Mark's lower lip before drawing by.

"By the way, while I was getting Amber and the kids settled in your house, Christy asked if you and I were dating."

Mark blinked.

"She what?"

"Do they know about your sexuality?"

"Never brought it up. It's not exactly something I'm going to discuss with them at their age." Mark swallowed. "Damn. Was she angry?"

"Curious, if anything. She said she already knew you preferred guys as she had seen how we interacted in the past. She just assumed we were dating in secret because we didn't want to upset her and Stevie."

Mark's expression had been very much like Jack's when she first said it. He hadn't realized the two of them had been so obvious. Mark licked his lips.

"What did you say to her?"

"I couldn't say anything immediately." Jack grimaced. "I mean, it's barely been twenty-four hours since you and I first got into bed. I know we discussed it, but I don't know what's set in stone."

Mark chuckled.

"You don't think what we said earlier about me wanting to be there for you if you needed me classified as official?"

"It could be, but…"

"No buts about it." Mark grabbed Jack's head and kissed him. "I'm in love with you, Jack. And I'd happily make this official for us, but only if you want it."

He loved him. Those words Jack had wanted to hear. That had Jack smiling. If Mark weren't in bed recovering from surgery, Jack would have jumped him.

"I like the sound of that. A lot." He sniggered and nipped at Mark's lower lip with his teeth. "I just hope you can cope with me. I am... Well, I do things big."

As he spoke, he took Mark's hand and pressed it over his erection, which was straining hard against his zipper. Mark grinned.

"I noticed. Although maybe not here. I don't want us to get thrown out."

"Later, then?"

"Oh, yeah." Mark was still smiling as Jack's lips brushed across his. "Definitely."

Printed in Great Britain
by Amazon